# The Esfah Sagas:
# Chill Wind

By
## Joseph W. Joiner

With revisions by
## Christopher D. Schmitz

## A Dragon Dice Novel

PUBLISHED BY TREESHAKER BOOKS

# THE ESFAH SAGAS

Rise and Fall of the Obsidian Grotto

Cast of Fate


*The Relic Quests*

Ashes of Ailushurai

Rise of the Champions (coming 2021)

Drakuwar (coming soon)


*The Cyrean Songs*

Chill Wind

Eye of the Storm

Secrets of the Shadowlands (coming 2021)

# STAY UP TO DATE ON THE WORLD OF ESFAH!

Get a free copy of book 1 in the Esfah Sagas by visiting:

www.subscribepage.com/getfreedragondicenovels

Subscribers who sign up for this no-spam email list will get free books, exclusive content, and more! You'll get *Rise & Fall of the Obsidian Grotto* immediately… if you would like more details or want to follow the author, you can find his details at the end of this book.

# BACKGROUND

Dragon Dice™ was originally created by Lester Smith and produced by TSR in 1995.It is an Origins Award winning strategy game where players create mythical armies using dice to represent each troop and is one of several collectible dice games that emerged in the 1990s. The game combines strategy and skill as well as a little luck.

After several years, TSR, now owned by Wizards of the Coast, had put Dragon Dice™ on hold to work on other projects. In October of 2000, SFR Inc. purchased the rights to Dragon Dice™.

Most of the races and monsters in original TSR Dragon Dice were created by Lester Smith and include some creatures unique to a fantasy setting and others that are familiar to the Dungeons & Dragons role-playing game. While the world of Esfah, where Dragon Dice™ takes place, has many similarities to that of Dungeons & Dragons, it is distinctly different in many respects. In some ways, there are greater unknowns and its history is both newer and older all at once.

Around the end of 1995 I was a teenager and avid board gamer who had a burger slinging job (which gave me a disposable income) and a car (that took most of my disposable income.) In addition to many other games I played as part of a regular quartet of gamers, Dragon Dice™ was one that we all enjoyed.

I fondly remember how the four of us would cut out of elective classes, study halls, and independent learning periods to meet up for gaming sessions. Dragon Dice™ came in a pocketable carrying bag which made it perfect for that.

We also had a mutual acquaintance. An older gentleman in town owned a new and used bookstore that also carried a limited supply of gaming products. Though he did not stock Dragon Dice™, he had a copy of *Cast of Fate*, the first Dragon Dice™ novel which included a special promo die; I snapped it up right away as the most avid reader of the foursome (which lent itself to me become the dedicated DM for our role-playing game sessions and solidified my path as a story-teller.) The included promotional die was our bright and shiny object for months.

*Cast of Fate* by Allen Varney was not the only book set in the world of Esfah, though it remains one of the few. As I write and publish more and more fiction (both Fantasy and Science Fiction,) I tend to write the stories that I've always wanted to… and I've always wanted to have a voice in a shared universe. Creating a story within the Dragon Dice™ universe is something I've always wanted to do, so I give a special thanks to SFR, a company composed of true and like-minded fans who have kept alive a product that was one of the gems of the 1990s.

—Chris

# FOREWORD

In eons past, when time was young and creation malleable, the four powers of Nature -- earth, air, fire, and water -- the children of Nature, gods in their own rights, brought forth two races of beings to care for their fledgling world, created by the all-father, Tarvenehl. One race, the selumari or coral elves, was created to husband the fluid forces of air and water. The other race, the vagha, a dwarvish race, embodied the stability of earth and the tempering power of fire. Together, these two peoples worked to nurture their infant world into something glorious and beautiful.

But Nature had a nemesis in Death, the spirit of entropy. In imitation of Nature, Death brought into being its own races: the morehl, or lava elves, who worshiped fire and destruction, and the trogs, a race of goblins, who sprang from earth and corruption. From the moment of their creation, the morehl and trogs sowed conflict, defiling the very world that gave them life and corrupting the other races who tended it. War sparked over land and possessions. Soon, hordes of dispossessed selumari, vagha, morehl, and trogs swept back and forth across the lands of Esfah, locked in endless battle.

In their struggles for supremacy over the fledgling world, the First Races pressed other magical beings into their service. The morehl were the first to do so, bringing up fire-breathing hellhounds and web-casting driders from the deepest caverns below Esfah. The trogs followed suit, leading trolls, harpies, and other monsters into battle. In response, the selumari called forth coral giants from the ocean and swarms of sprites from the skies.

The vagha enlisted gargoyles, androsphinxes, and other creatures of the crags.

Conflict raged across the face of Esfah, and Death delighted in the carnage.

Back and forth across the world, darkness battle against light. Each side pushed harder yet for victory and the battles grew ever savage and desperate. New races arose, each pressed into the fray of the bloody struggle that seemed to have no end in sight.

Saddened by the bloodshed, Nature, the goddess-mother Ghaeial, dealt death to preserve life. Death, the bastard child Malgrimm – son of Ghaeial and Selurehl, the god known as Void – reveled in the chaos, terror, and pain that war brought.

A time of champions arose to safeguard the realm. Wars continued and an entire age passed. Pockets of tenuous peace grew from apathy – a new trick engineered by Death to soften the resolve of Nature's troops, almost seeming to abandon his playground for the comforts of the Abyss – but his attention never truly waned.

Esfah has never known true peace. It is not in the planet's makeup: this is where the children of gods war on their behalf. Both old and new races struggle ever onward – creatures inspired to greater ends, forever in search of either an end to the bloodshed, or carnage renewed, as each is bent towards his or her own ends.

Esfah cannot know peace. Malgrimm, the god known as Death, will not allow it. Only a few know his true name – and to speak it aloud is to court Death himself.

For a short video overview of Esfah's origins, visit

https://youtu.be/JhF8RPFkF9I

For up to date information on the world of Esfah, and all things related to the Dragon Dice universe, including products and specials, check out:

http://www.sfr-inc.com

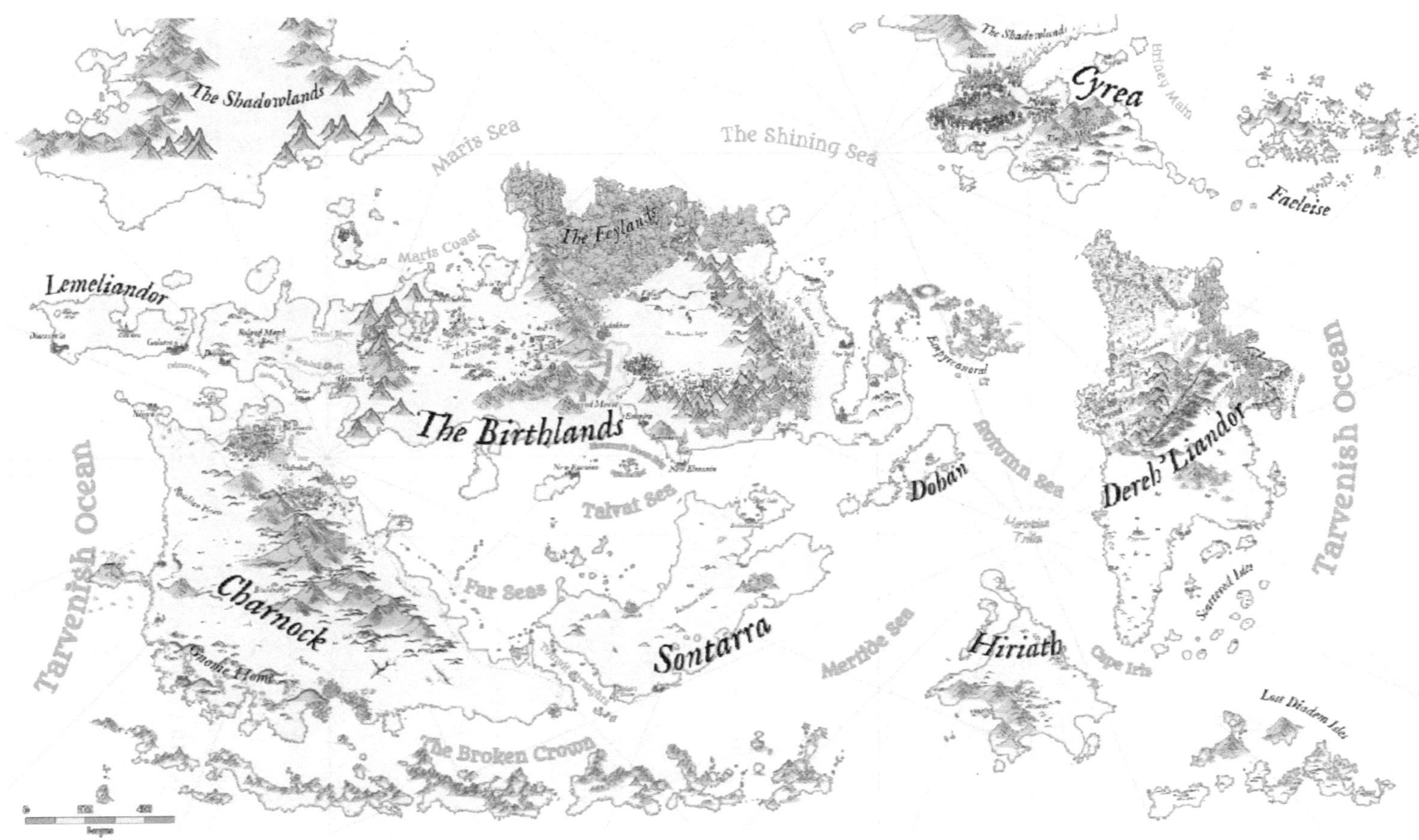
The Shadowlands
Cyrea
Pitney Main
Faeleise
The Shining Sea
Maris Sea
The Feylands
Maris Coast
Lemeliandor
Tarvenish Ocean
The Birthlands
Dereb'Liandor
Tarvenish Ocean
Talvat Sea
Doban
Autumn Sea
Charnock
Far Seas
Sontarra
Meritle Sea
Hiriath
Cape Iris
Scattered Isles
Gnome Home
The Broken Crown
Last Diadem Isles

## ACKNOWLEDGEMENTS
## AND
## DEDICATION

In his original dedication Joseph Joiner, author, thanked Chuck & Pat Pint, Clifford and Tiffany Wiggs, Steven, Jonathan and Robert Braun, Dave Pint, and all those at SFR, Inc. for their wonderful support through the years, permission to write the story, not to mention thousands of dice and countless battles both in person and online.

"I could not have done this without all of you.

Very special thanks to my friend **Steve Braun** for the Magestorm riddle when I was having a serious mental cramp and unable to come up with anything.

You helped me finish the story, bud!

The author would also like to thank the following people for the time they gave me proofreading and critiquing the story.

Jose and Jenny Balderrama Steven Braun Jennifer Leigh Evans Joseph P. Joiner Paula D. Joiner Ed Meredith Chris Ponton Tamara Mabe Ponton Robert Radcliffe William Roberts Janette Romero Amy & Wes Schulmeister Cliff and Tiffany Wiggs."

In memory of my father, M.L. "Skeet" Joiner (1925-2007), and to my daughter, Jennifer Leigh Evans.

Thanks, Dad, for always believing in me and teaching me to persevere by cutting out the middle-man and going directly to the top to get what I want! I wish you could be here to see this.

Thank you, Jennifer, for your constant encouragement and love. You are my greatest creation.

This story is also dedicated to all the fans of Dragon Dice all over the world, who kept the game going since 1994, and also to the guys at SFR, Inc., for their tireless efforts and contributions to the game since acquiring it.

Roughly a decade after Joe Joiner released this story, the literary world of Esfah finally comes into its own. I would like to think that he would have been extremely excited to see where it is going and participate further in it.

Sadly, he passed away in 2014. While I never had the chance to meet Joe, I am pleased to see his enthusiasm and excitement for the world of Esfah and feel that we may have been kindred spirits. I would like to dedicate this version of Chill Wind to Joe, his legacy, and to the Joiner family.

—Christopher D. Schmitz

# PART I

*"The truest friendship is born of a noble heart."*
—*King Walen sa'Desmon the True, The Cyrean Songs
698 SA*

The moon was full and low in the evening sky as Geril made his way along the rocky path toward home. His battle-axe swung at his side, but his steps were the slow tread of weariness. He stopped for a moment and leaned against a large boulder near the path. He uncorked his waterskin and took a long drink to wash the dust of travel from his throat. Not far now, he thought.

Another few hours would see him feasting in the great hall of Balgavarr with his friends and family. He sighed as he glanced down at the axe. The blade was nicked and scarred, but still deadly sharp, like the warrior that wielded it.

How long had it been? Four months since the selumari forces fighting near Tulgesh had sent a message asking for help. The council had been convened, and though relations with the coral elves were strained, the decision to aid them was quickly made. The morehl and trogs had invaded far too much territory in the last two years, and the threat was growing greater for his own people, the vagha. The lava elves had made no secret of their coveting of Balgavarr Reaches. To allow them to conquer Matrek's forces at Tulgesh would be practically opening a door and inviting them in.

Another swallow of water, and another memory. Two hundred dwarven warriors had marched or ridden from Balgavarr, the cavalry mounted on their mammoths and lizards, marching behind the infantry of axes and crossbows.

A tenday later they were in the thick of the fighting, and Geril had watched his friends die. The forces of Death had laughed in glee as the morehl had shattered the organized squadron of selumari and vagha. What had been a brilliant defense strategy was rendered useless by the appearance of a score of driders, the hideous mixture of elf and spider. The troops had nearly frozen in fear as the monsters fell upon them, their swords and crossbows forgotten as they were decimated.

Geril smiled sadly as he remembered how his comrades had risen fearlessly against the beasts, their axes severing legs and their crossbow bolts inflicting mortal wounds. The great mammoths had trampled many of the driders, but the sticky webs of the monsters slowed and even stopped the beasts and allowed morehl soldiers to use their spears to bring down the noble steeds. The fearlessness of the vagha inspired the elves to rally, and the day was nearly saved. But the damage was already done. The remnants of the selumari and vagha armies had been pushed back, and Tulgesh was abandoned to the enemy who now occupied it.

Geril corked his waterskin and started walking again. While the vagha forces had been cut nearly in half, they had deemed it their duty to stay with the elves in case the morehl decided to hunt them down and finish them off.

Matrek had been grateful, but had insisted that a messenger be sent immediately to inform Balgavarr of all that had occurred. Secretly, Geril wondered if this was an attempt by Matrek to secure more dwarven warriors to his cause. He had been selected to go, and now, nearly a tenday later, he was nearly home.

A hundred paces later, he realized that the warm spring breeze had suddenly grown cold, and that the normal sounds of the wilderness were hushed and silent. His axe was in his hands in the space of a thought, his warrior's instincts for survival momentarily taking control. He looked around cautiously. Nothing moved, but still he sensed that not all was right. He took a few more steps, making no sound.

Something growled up the mountain slope to his left, and he whirled around, axe raised and ready. In the darkness, he could see a pair of glowing red eyes. He backed away, but whatever it was did not follow. He moved to the left, and the eyes tracked him. He took another step forward, and was rewarded with a long hiss, enough to make him retreat. "Who is that?" he called softly. "I warn you, I am weary, but still strong enough to defend myself." No answer came, but he could now hear rough breathing, the kind any creature would make when injured. He lowered the axe. "Are you in need of help? I have water."

"Waaa-t-rrrr. Y-esssss," said a voice. The eyes blinked and turned away. Geril unhooked the waterskin from his belt and tossed it gently toward where he had last seen movement. Now he picked up the sound of something large moving in the darkness, and then the sounds of the last of his water being swallowed in two great gulps. A moment later the empty skin thumped to the ground near his feet. He retrieved it, pleased to note that the cork had been replaced instead of carelessly discarded. "Can I do more for you?" he called. "The dwarves are not without knowledge of healing, and I have some small skill."

Several moments passed, then the thick, raspy voice said, "Cooomme."

Geril lowered his axe and shrugged off his pack. "I'll need my lantern to see better. Will the light bother you?"

"Liiiight? Noooo. Briiiing liiight." Geril frowned. Bring the lantern or not? The creature's words could be taken either way. Still, he needed to see.

Using a spell taught to him by the warrior wizard Latkis on the march to Tulgesh, he conjured a small flame to the lantern wick. Closing the hood, he raised the wick, and the deepening night was suddenly filled with a warm golden glow. He then turned toward the mysterious figure and gasped.

The beast was huge, and like nothing he had ever seen. It resembled a mountain lion, except he had never seen a cat so muscular. Glossy blue-black fur covered most of it. It was heavily muscled and powerful in appearance, an altogether imposing creature, but it was the immense bat-like wings attached to its shoulders that he stared at in wonder. This was a creature of the air! He approached slowly, lantern in one hand, the other held out palm up. He would make no sudden moves where this beast was concerned.

"Are you injured?" The great red eyes blinked, as if the creature were pondering the words. It slowly nodded its head. With a groan, it twisted its body until he could see the wound between its massive shoulders. Taking another step closer, he could see it had been caused by a morehl pistol. The ball had not penetrated deeply; he could see it just below the puckered edge of the wound. This creature must have skin like stone to have taken such a hit and not been killed.

"I'm coming closer," Geril warned. "I'm going to try to help you."

The great head nodded again, then lowered to the ground, where the eyes closed. Geril moved around the creature, being careful to avoid stepping on the wings, which were thin and leathery. He knelt and examined the wound. "Do you have a name?" he asked. "I am Geril, son of Ghuren. I am from Balgavarr Reaches." Taking out his dagger, he used the same spell that had lit his lantern to make the blade hot.

"Thraaaag," said the voice.

"Thrag? Well, Thrag, I wish I could say this wasn't going to hurt, but unfortunately it is. I hope you'll forgive me." As carefully as he could, Geril placed his fingers around the wound, blinking in surprise when he felt that the flesh beneath them was cool to the touch. Then he inserted the blade into the wound, working the tip of the dagger down and under the ball. Yellow pus leaked from the wound and hissed as it made contact with the hot blade.

The wound had been festering for days. Thrag however, bore it with stoicism, barely flinching as Geril probed the wound.

Feeling that the blade was under the ball, Geril quickly applied pressure and popped it out of the wound. Thrag shuddered and moaned, baring long, sharp teeth. Geril winced and prepared to flee in case Thrag turned on him.

Thrag simply lay back down and growled softly.

The dwarf acted as gentle as possible. "I'm going to have to close this. Since I left my needle and thread at home, I'll have to use fire. Hold still."

Concentrating, Geril channeled that same fire spell into the now bleeding wound. Thrag arched his back and hissed loudly. Steam rose from the wound. When Geril blinked and leaned back, he saw that the wound had closed. It would scab over and heal. It would probably be sore for a few days, but he reasoned that Thrag would hardly notice. "There my friend," he said, "that should be better."

He stood and walked back to his pack. Carrying it back to Thrag, he opened it and dug for some of his rations. Some dried meat and a few pieces of fruit were all that remained, but he offered them to Thrag. If he got out of this alive, he could gorge himself upon reaching his father's home. What was a few hours' hunger compared to that? A hand as large as his head took the offered food, and Geril couldn't help but wince at the size of the talons on that hand.

Thrag chewed slowly, his eyes watching Geril almost thoughtfully.

Then the hand lifted slowly, and reached for the dwarf. One razor sharp talon poked Geril gently on the chest. "Maa-aaan?"

Geril grinned. "No," he said, "not a man. My people are called the vagha. The other races call us dwarves." He pointed to the north, toward Balgavarr. "We live there, in the mountains."

Thrag's eyes looked to where the dwarf pointed. The peaks were just visible as the moonlight reflected off the snow-capped summits. Geril would have sworn that there was an expression of longing on the hairy face. Then Thrag seemed to sigh. At least that's what Geril thought it was. It sounded more like a growl. "Yessss," Thrag said. "Hooooome."

Geril blinked. "You come from the mountains?"

Thrag looked back at him and nodded again. "Hooome," he said.

"Well. my large friend. We must see that you get back there. Can you walk?"

Thrag blinked slowly, and then tried to sit up. Muscles trembled as he struggled to rise, but fell back down, exhausted. Geril frowned. So much for a hot meal and a warm bed this night. He looked up to see Thrag watching him, and he smiled and shrugged. "Don't worry, Thrag. I'll stay with you tonight. Maybe you'll be stronger in the morning." He stood and stretched, then jumped as Thrag roared.

He stumbled away; wondering what he had done wrong. Thrag was watching him again, mouth hanging open, panting. Geril expected rage, but instead realized Thrag was worried about being left alone. He held up his hands and grinned. "I'm just going to set some traps. Maybe we can get something more filling to eat." Thrag's mouth closed, and he settled down again, but Geril swore the beast still looked worried. "I'll be back. I promise," he said. He was about to turn and go when another thought crossed his mind. He went back to his pack and pulled out his largest blanket. Unfolding it, he spread as much of it as he could over Thrag. "Rest easy, friend. I'll return soon." With that, he moved into the night.

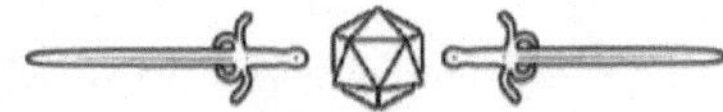

Geril awoke with the sun shining full in his face and opened his eyes to find a dozen swords at his throat. The morehl surrounded him. By the beard of Eldurim, what were they doing this far north? "On your feet, dwarf!" said the tallest one, who also held his axe. Geril looked around for Thrag, but the winged monster was gone. He stood slowly, wondering where the big beast had gone.

Hands grabbed him, forcing his arms up behind his back. "Well, well, well," the tall one said. "I thought vagha hated sleeping out of doors."

"There's always an exception. I thought morehl couldn't stand the cold of these northern regions."

"Balgavarr Reaches is a tempting morsel. We'll be warm enough there once you show us the way."

"I'll die first." The thought of these raiders wandering the streets of Balgavarr was frightening.

The lava elf grinned wickedly. "That can be arranged," he said. "but you will show us where the entrance to Balgavarr lies before you die."

"Never!" shouted Geril, suddenly thrusting forward, his dwarven strength breaking the hold of the elves restraining him. He lowered his head and rammed the leader full in the stomach, bowling them both over. The other elves cried out and leapt to the rescue. Geril fought wildly, his fists striking out, the fury within him fueling the inner fires of his rage. It wasn't enough though. Soon they had him overpowered and bound hand and foot.

Many of them were bleeding from the injuries he had caused. The leader had taken the brunt of the attack and showed the worst of it. His uniform was torn and dirty, and he was holding his ribs with one hand, and his broken nose with the other. "You're dead," he rasped, drawing his dagger.

Geril saw Death coming for him as the others lifted him to his feet. "It will be hard to find Balgavarr now," he laughed.

"We'll find it, anyway. Pull back his head. I'm going to cut him deep."

Cold steel touched his throat, and Geril closed his eyes and waited for oblivion. Then a roar shattered the quiet morning, and a cold wind rushed past him. The dagger at his throat vanished, as did the elf holding it. The hands that had been grasping him suddenly let go and he crashed face first to the earth.

Rolling over, he saw Thrag vaulting skyward, carrying the lead elf by the arms. The others had scattered in fear. The huge wings flapped as Thrag soared higher. The elf was screaming and kicking, struggling to free himself despite the horrendous drop. Thrag obliged him by ripping both arms from their sockets. The elf shrieked as he plummeted to the earth. He fell out of sight behind a hill, but the thick, wet sound of his landing still reached Geril's ears.

The crack of the lava elf pistols caused him to jump, and he cried out, "No!" He knew they were firing at Thrag, and hoped the brute was high enough to avoid the shots.

One of the morehl darted out from behind a rock, firing blindly as he sought better cover. Geril watched amazed as a spear of crystal ice impaled the elf. The morehl stumbled and fell dead. Geril looked up to see Thrag fly over, another sharp spear of ice forming from nothingness in his hand.

Another of the elves screamed as the spear crashed near him, shattering into a thousand sharp icy shards that flew into his face, cutting him in many places and effectively blinding him.

Thrag roared again as another volley of shots was fired at him. Geril shouted in triumph as his giant friend twisted in mid-air, avoiding the shots.

Then the wings tucked in as Thrag dove towards the earth, to unfold as he swooped into a graceful glide just above the ground. The remaining morehl had grouped together, and Thrag crashed into them with the force of a lightning strike, talons extended.

The battle was bloody, but brief. When it ended, Thrag stood on hind legs, panting heavily. The creature shook himself, then stomped over to Geril, his steps making the ground shake. With the ease a mother might carry an infant, Geril was lifted gently to his feet. Thrag used a talon to slice easily through the bonds, and Geril winced as blood flowed back into his limbs. He looked up at Thrag and grinned. "Thank you my friend," he said, "but what took you so long?"

Thrag growled softly and patted Geril on the head. "Hooome?"

"Yes," Geril agreed. "It's time to go home. I must warn my people that the morehl are in the land. We must prepare. You should go home as well."

The dwarf retrieved his axe and pack, then turned to Thrag. "My road lies this way. I know not where your home lies, but I wish you safe travel."

Thrag strode over. Staring down at Geril, he thumped the dwarf on the chest. "Thraaaag go Gerilll hooome."

Geril's jaw dropped. "You want to come with me? To my home?"

Thrag nodded excitedly. Geril laughed out loud. "What will my father think of you? Come then, my friend. We travel together." He turned and started down the path, the seed of an impossible idea planted in his mind.

Suddenly two strong hands grabbed him around the middle, and there was a sudden rush of wind as Thrag took to the air. Geril gulped as the earth fell away beneath them. He pointed one shaky hand to the north, and a distant peak. "That way, Thrag!" he called. "There lies Balgavarr!"

Thrag banked gently, flying swiftly towards the distant peaks. Geril could not help but think of the reception they would receive. It was sure to be a memorable one.

The sentries in the watchtowers spotted them first, sending out cries of alarm as Thrag winged down from the sky to land gently near the hidden entrance to the mountain city. Geril sent a grateful prayer to Eldurim and Firiel for his safe deliverance, and the fact that Thrag had not dropped him.

Once on the ground, he turned and patted the broad, hairy chest, adding a scratch for good measure. Thrag panted and let out a small cheerful bark.

They were suddenly surrounded by more than twenty archers and swordsmen. Thrag growled and swept Geril into an almost suffocating protective embrace, the great wings folding around the two bodies. "Easy, Thrag," he groaned. "They're my friends." The pressure eased as Thrag released him. The wings unfolded, and Geril stumbled into view of the warriors.

A cheer went up as he was recognized, and a moment later he was thronged on all sides by old friends asking questions. They were very curious about Thrag, who watched quizzically. "What is it?" asked Taness, Geril's nephew.

Geril looked over his shoulder at Thrag, who was enduring a mob of curious onlookers who were touching him hesitantly, and staring in open-mouthed wonder. The dwarven warrior was surprised at how quickly he had grown fond of the powerful beast. "He's a friend," he said.

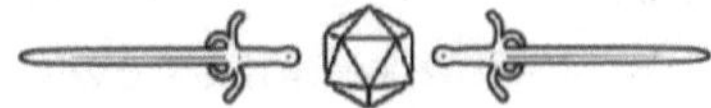

The Council immediately convened to hear Geril's story and to see Thrag for themselves. The mighty beast was content to sit in a corner of the Council chamber and gnaw on a bone while they discussed him. Geril quickly grew weary of the question-and-answer session. The story of the battle at Tulgesh brought equal amounts of anger and anguish, but the morehl scouting party into their lands was met with disbelief and even fury.

Thrag's silent presence added weight to what might have been an unbelievable tale. The Council at last turned their attention to Geril's newfound companion. Most were unable to figure out just what manner of creature he was. Then Geril's father, Ghuren, stood. "I believe I know what this creature may be," he said. The attention of the Council and all present were immediately focused on the elder vagha.

"The old legends speak of a time when the forces of Death sought new allies in the war for Esfah. In the bleak and bitter cold mountains of the Shadowlands, the spirit of darkness made creatures from the black ice of the mountains. These bat-like creatures were to be the mightiest of Death's warriors, but their hearts were not as cold as the ice they were made of. They craved not the violence of their maker, so the dark spirit abandoned his creation, thinking they would perish without its guiding presence.

"But the creatures survived and even flourished in a region where nothing lived. Unknown to all of the races, they venture rarely into the lowlands, lest they be seen by their maker, who might destroy them.

"They named themselves, frostwings. The *Book of the Land* has historically called them the areosa."

The words were absorbed by all, and eventually every eye in the chamber was on Thrag, who seemed oblivious to all and contentedly sucked the marrow from the leg bone he had been gnawing. Then bedlam broke out as everyone began speaking at once. Only Geril remained calm and silent, waiting for the outcome. He stood next to Thrag, idly scratching his brutish friend behind the ears. Thrag yawned and stretched out full length on the tile floor.

Most of the conversation that reached Geril was concerned with whether this newly discovered race was a threat to the forces of Nature. The fact that Thrag had shown no sign of violence factored strongly in the debate.

Geril waited as long as he could, but saw that they were getting nowhere. It was time for action. He strode out into the center of the chamber, Thrag getting up and following him. He held up his hands for silence and was completely ignored. "Your pardon, everyone…" he began, but again, no one noticed his presence.

Thrag however, did notice. He opened his mouth and roared.

Silence.

"Thank you, Thrag," Geril chuckled. He turned to the assembly.

"Councilors, have we forgotten that the morehl are intruding into our lands? While Thrag here is an exciting discovery, the weightier matter is the fact that our home here is threatened by the agents of Death."

"Geril speaks truly!" called out Rannon, leader of the Wizards Guild.

"The morehl have always wanted Balgavarr Reaches, they've made no secret of that. Should we ignore their presence until it's too late? I say not!"

Geril nodded in agreement. "Exactly," he said. "You have heard me say that Tulgesh has fallen to the morehl and trog hordes. How long before they discover Balgavarr's entrance?

We've always been strong, but never strong enough. Together the selumari and vagha have fended off the advances of the morehl and trogs into our territories. Only together have we held them back. Now Tulgesh is gone, and the elves have fled into the surrounding wilderness or taken to the seas. How long before our enemies find us?" He paused to allow the words to sink in. He then turned to Thrag, patting the shaggy hide affectionately. "I say to you now, perhaps we have found a new ally."

"What is one beast against an army?" said Vors, leader of the Council.

"You said yourself he was wounded and near death when you found him."

"True," Geril conceded. "But he fought against a dozen of them the next morning and emerged unscathed. He flies as swiftly as an eagle and is stronger than ten of us together. Ghuren has said that perhaps he is only one of many, let us ask their aid against the morehl."

"Maybe he's the last of his kind," Vors challenged.

Geril shrugged. "That could be. But if he is not, imagine the hearts of our enemies when they see death falling on them from the sky. I say we seek their help."

Thrag took that moment to rise to his full height above Geril. The frostwing warrior spread his arms and opened his hands. The air above his palms sparkled as it crystallized into long, razor sharp spears of solid ice.

Without warning, the spears were flung against the wall of the chamber, sinking into the solid stone fully half their length.

Those watching were stunned. Thrag lowered himself and gently laid his heavy hand on Geril's shoulder. The dwarf's knees buckled a bit under the weight, but he steadied himself. Thrag's voice then resonated throughout the chamber. Deep and throaty, it filled the hall. "Weeee… help."

# PART 2

*"Adventure always finds those that do not seek it."*
*—Zephras Thunderfist, vaghan hero 829 SA*

Two days later, Geril was packing when Ghuren knocked on the doorframe of his son's bedroom. The elder vagha found a chair and sat down heavily. "Ah," he said, "these old bones of mine, how they creak louder with each passing year." He rubbed his legs and looked at his son. "You are certain you wish to do this? Another journey so soon after the last one?"

Geril paused. "Every day we hesitate is another day wasted against the morehl. Many of our people are in hiding with the selumari, father. I cannot forget them, or those that died the last day of the battle. Thrag's people may very well turn the tide of this war and maybe drive out the lava elves completely."

Ghuren sighed. "You place much hope on the frostwings, my son. They may very well deny you despite Thrag's offer. He could be just a common soldier, unable to make decisions for the rest of his kind."

"It's still worth the risk, Father. We must take the chance."

"It would seem easier to simply call our people home, seal the entrance to our mountain, and leave the selumari to their fate. The morehl might not find it."

Geril gave his father a scalding glance, and Ghuren held up his hand. "I know what you're thinking. While the truce between our peoples may be shaky, we are both the children of Nature. We cannot abandon them."

Geril sighed and almost smiled, the corners of his mouth turning up a bit. "I should know better than to question my father's words," he said.

"That's true," Ghuren said, causing his son to chuckle. "I worry, though. Thrag has proven his friendship to you, but to many of us, he remains a beast. A creature of legend come to life, to be sure, and something to be held in awe, but still a fierce creature, no matter how tame he may appear."

The young dwarf closed his pack. He was wondering where this talk was headed. "He saved my life, Father. My head would be a trophy on a morehl pike right now if not for him. Let's not forget that."

"Of course not," Ghuren agreed. "I will be forever grateful to Thrag for that, as well as to his people if they come to our aid. Forgive me if I place so little hope on the frostwings, my son. We've been promised help before, remember?"

Geril nodded. "The amazons," he said softly, remembering events of seven years before. The morehl had encroached into the territory of the vagha, searching again for Balgavarr Reaches. Their army had been vast, and the vagha had cowered within their mountain home knowing that if they were discovered, their army could never stand against such a force without aid.

An envoy had been sent to the humans and the selumari to beg their aid against the morehl. The coral elves had come at once, marching without delay to the home of their allies. The warrior women had heard the pleas of the dwarves, and their war chief promised to send troops. The morehl had continued to advance, using the trogs to take the brunt of the defenses of the selumari and vagha.

The battle had been bloody for both sides, and only the combined magic of the elven enchanters and dwarf wizards had sent the enemy fleeing. The earth magic of the dwarves had turned the ground beneath the morehl and trogs to mud, where they sank helplessly. The selumari enchanters had then called down lightning from a clear sky. The strikes had killed dozens of soldiers. The soldiers of Nature had been on the brink of madness due to the illusionary flames cast by the morehl necromancers.

Many of them had fled in panic. The necromancer had been laughing in fiendish glee when the bolt of lightning split him in half. Once that threat and the death magic were gone, the morehl lost their edge. Victory in that battle had been assured. Not one of the lava elves had escaped. The promised assistance of the amazons had never appeared.

Messages sent to the humans had not been answered, and more messengers had been sent to the plains of Seshara. They found the homeland of the amazons in the hands of the morehl. The city of Thurisa was silent and empty. Whatever had happened to the humans remained an unsolved puzzle.

Geril could understand his father's uncertainty towards the Frostings. "I trust Thrag, father." *I'm not sure why, but I do.* "He's intelligent, we've already seen that. I'm sure he would not speak for his people unless he was certain of their aid."

"I hope you're right," Ghuren said with a sigh. "Too many of our best warriors have died already, and the morehl seem only to grow stronger." He stood and walked to the door. Reaching around out of sight, he grunted as if lifting something heavy. Geril was unable to hide his surprise as Ghuren's axe came into view. The handle had been worked smooth again and polished with chubba berry juice until it shone. The blade had also been reworked. The scars and gouges were gone from the edge, and it had been sharpened until it was razor fine. "A few years ago I wielded this with the best of our warriors. Now, it grows too heavy." He handed the weapon to his son. "I pray you find the answers we need, Geril. I would rather see this hung in a place of honor, rather than one of memorial." He embraced his son, and Geril was stunned to find that the elder dwarf was no longer the stocky warrior of times long gone, but rather a thin and frail mockery of that once great soldier. Then Ghuren was gone without another word.

Geril shrugged on his pack and grabbed his axe. It suddenly seemed much heavier.

Many of the vaghan community, including the elders, were there to see them off. They had gathered at the same courtyard where the two adventurers had landed just days ago. While open to the air, the courtyard was still well hidden, and was all but invisible to anyone or anything that did not know what to look for. The children had discovered that Thrag was gentle despite his great size and monstrous appearance and were gathered around the brute, scratching and tickling the glossy hide. Geril chuckled as Thrag seemed to purr in contentment. Upon seeing his friend, Thrag slowly stood, so as not to frighten the children, and called softly, "Gerr-elll." It seemed his command of language was improving. Geril strode over and patted Thrag's broad chest.

"Are you ready to go home, my big friend?"

"Hooome," Thrag growled. "Yesss."

Elder Vors appeared and grasped Geril's arm. "Be swift," he said. "We cannot afford further delays. Another morehl scouting party has been seen. We fear they have found their comrades, and once word of that is known, they will come here and search until they find us. It is no longer a matter of aiding the selumari. Now it is our very survival."

Geril nodded as he shrugged off the hand that gripped him. His gut churned from the news and at being so close to an elder he despised. Vors almost always opposed Ghuren in council matters. Two days. In just two days the lava elves had found the remains of the scouts Thrag had killed and were no doubt returning with all haste to their leaders. That could only mean a larger unseen force was in the region. It would not be long before

Balgavarr was discovered. "I give you my word, Elder. We will not dally."

A great weight seemed to lift from the elder's shoulders. "That is well," he said, and turned away. This left room for those who had gathered to come and say their own goodbyes. Geril was amazed at the number of people that wished to say a few words and touch both him and Thrag. *They see us as their last hope*, he realized. *Firiel and Eldurim help us all if I'm wrong about the frostwings.*

When the well-wishers had at last stepped back, with some gentle prodding by Vors and other elders, Thrag lowered himself so that Geril could climb onto his shoulders. The dwarf leaned over and whispered into one of Thrag's ears, "Give them hope, my friend. Show your strength," he said, wondering if he would be understood.

Thrag rose to his full height, his dark wings billowing out to either side as he spread his arms and roared to the clear morning sky. The vagha stepped back in surprise and then began to cheer as Thrag vaulted skyward. His wings caught the air, and they rose easily. From high above, Geril looked down on the hidden courtyard. He could just make out the opening and a few people waving. His heart thudded in his chest, and he was suddenly very lonely. He quelled the emotion. He would be home soon enough, leading an army unlike any seen before. They would drive out the lava elves and goblins, and Balgavarr and Tulgesh would at last know peace.

"Fly, Thrag!" he cried. "Show me your home!"

The frostwing bellowed in answer and banked away from Balgavarr toward the north and west. Geril could see snow-capped peaks ahead and was grateful he had thought to pack his cold weather gear.

Swift as an eagle despite his great size, Thrag flew straight as an arrow toward the icy cliffs of the Shadowlands. *A grand adventure*, Geril thought. *I only hope we return in time.*

The novelty of flight was quick to wear off. The closer they flew to the northern mountains, the colder the air became, and Geril was unable to get to his pack for a coat while holding on to Thrag's neck. The northern woods of the Dur'sona were still covered with the last of the winter snow. He had watched with curiosity as they passed over the thick woods. It was whispered that the efflorah resided there. The treefolk were creatures of legend and were thought to be reclusive, seeking to avoid the other races. None of them had ever been seen. Of course, no one went looking for them either. Yet those who did venture among the trees did so with blades covered and went without fire until they emerged. To do otherwise was to tempt fate. Lifting his hands, he rubbed his cheeks. His face felt numb, and there was ice in his mustache and beard. Only his hands remained warm, buried as they were in Thrag's thick fur.

They'd been flying for hours, yet the frostwing warrior seemed tireless. His breathing sounded rougher, but at this altitude even a highland dwarf like Geril was gasping for breath. He closed his eyes and allowed himself to be lulled by the wind and the movement of Thrag's wings. He jerked them open when he felt himself going to sleep, grabbing for purchase in Thrag's coat.

As for Thrag, he felt his rider almost slip. While Geril was perfectly safe (Thrag would never allow him to fall, at least not too far), the frostwing warrior knew that Geril was tiring, and needed rest. He began a slow descent. They were still low enough in the mountains for there to be trees, and Thrag picked a small clearing among a stand of pines. There, he knew, Geril could make a fire and warm himself.

The ground seemed to rise with heart stopping speed to the dwarf, and for a brief moment he wondered if there was something wrong with Thrag. Then he felt the wings beat even harder, and Thrag's legs extended to absorb the shock of their landing. It took only a few steps to stop, and Thrag lowered himself again so that Geril could clamber off his back.

The dwarf stood on shaky legs, glad to be on solid ground again. He looked around the clearing. "Is this it?" he asked.

Thrag shook his head. "Nooo. Gerr-el ressst." The dwarf slumped gratefully as Thrag scratched out a dry spot in the snow.

When he had cleared out a large area, Geril happily stamped his boots free of snow. "Thank you," he said, and began gathering twigs and dried leaves for a fire. From his pack he removed the totem given him by Latkis.

The sightstone allowed him a small use of magic. He could have tapped its power without taking it out, but the stone was beautiful. To anyone else, it appeared as nothing more than a good-sized garnet that barely covered his palm. Why he had been entrusted with it was something he still pondered.

Most pieces of magical equipment were reserved for use by wizards, or the thaumaturgists and theurgists. In all things magical, they were notoriously stingy. He shivered as the power of Firiel flowed through him, igniting the small pile of twigs. Sometimes he wondered if maybe he should have apprenticed himself to the Wizards' Guild. Latkis had said he had the aptitude. Ghuren had quashed the idea firmly. For generations, his ancestors had been warriors.

Geril would not break that tradition. He placed the sightstone back in his pack, wondering idly how such a wondrous thing came to be.

With the fire burning brightly, the ice was finally melting from his beard. Warm again, he took some dried meat from his pack, speared it with a sharp twig, and then propped it over the flames to heat it. He then changed into his warmer clothes while his meal cooked. Despite being early afternoon, the sky was overcast and dark, with small, stinging particles of ice blowing in the breeze. The trees surrounding the clearing bore a thin coat of ice and snow. Geril looked around as he warmed himself. He wondered if any of his people had ever been this deep in the Shadowlands before.

"Are we near your home?" he asked Thrag.

The frostwing blew a cloud of steam from his nostrils. "Not farrr," he growled, eyeing the hunk of meat Geril was roasting over the small flames.

The dwarf noticed the stare and fished out another piece from his pack. He tossed it to Thrag, who snatched it out of the air with his mouth.

Geril continued to look around while he ate. The land was bleak beyond any he had ever seen. The swampland of the trogs could almost be called hospitable compared to this. He shivered inside his thick coat. The vagha were used to the warm embrace of the earth, not the cold whispers of the highland winds.

A few thin clouds crawled across a sky that glittered with millions of crystal snowflakes. Despite its harshness, he found it oddly beautiful. He picked up a rock the size of his fist and examined it. Small chunks of quartz shone in the heavy granite. Cold it may be, but Nature was still with him. He smiled as he caressed the stone. Eldurim and his sister Firiel were a part of him no matter where he traveled. Their strength was his strength. "I will succeed," he said softly. The stone fell to the ground. "Let's go, Thrag. I'm thawed enough." He stamped out the fire, then covered the ashes with snow to both smother and hide it — not that the morehl would likely come to this high country.

Despite their love of mountains, this cold would be too much for them.

Thrag waited patiently as Geril climbed to his broad shoulders. Once the dwarven warrior was seated firmly, they took to the air.

Geril jerked awake. He was lying on soft warm furs next to a small fire.

He sat up and felt around anxiously for his axe, exhaling heavily in relief when he felt the familiar smooth handle. Moving the furs aside, he smiled at the crescent blade, feeling a little sheepish that he could feel so comforted by the sight of a mere weapon. He strapped it to his back as he looked up. Where in Sha'la'dinan was he?

The last thing he could remember was Thrag flying away from the clearing in which they had stopped to rest. After several hours of flying, his eyes had become increasingly heavy. He would rest them just a moment.

Then he woke up here. There were two possible explanations. Either Thrag had placed him in this cave so he could rest, or they had reached the homelands of the areosa.

The cave was small. Small enough that the light from the fire was enough to illuminate all the rock walls around him. Across from him, a trickle of water ran down the wall from the ceiling and dripped into a shallow basin in the floor. Geril crawled to the tiny pool and dipped his hand into the cold water, wincing as he did so. How could the water be so cold without freezing over? He drank from his cupped hand; the water was so sweet and refreshing that he leaned over and drank right from the basin.

Looking up, he wiped his mouth on his sleeve as the walls caught his attention. Being a dwarf, he had a natural affinity for stone. His kind had lived within it for nigh countless generations. The wall he stared at, indeed the very cavern he sat in was not naturally formed. The walls were covered with deep cuts and gouges that no stonecutting tool could have possibly made. In fact, they looked to have been made by claws. He swallowed hard. What manner of creature could dig in solid rock with only its claws?

"Gerrril," a voice spoke from behind him.

Whirling around, he smiled at the sight of Thrag's shaggy face in the opening of the cave. The frostwing actually looked excited. "So, my large friend, have we reached your home?" Geril asked.

"Hooome? Yesss. Gerrril come." Feeling his pulse race as he moved to the opening, the dwarf lowered himself to his hands and knees as Thrag's head withdrew. Crawling through, he stood on a high ledge and gasped in awe at what he saw.

The cavern was immense. Formed of rock and ice, it stretched further than Geril could see. Massive dagger-like icicles hung from the ceiling of the cave. Far away to his right he could see the opening only because bright sunlight was shining through. The light struck the hanging icicles and lit the entire cavern as it was reflected. On the cavern walls was more ice, but strangely formed. It looked to have been smeared across the surface of the rock. It also reflected the sunlight, making the cave even brighter. Millions of rainbows danced everywhere. For creatures of such power, the frostwings lived in a place of cold and glorious beauty. Caves dotted the walls, and it was to and from these that hundreds of frostwings flew.

They filled the air of the cavern. Beautiful and graceful, their aerial dance was breathtaking. Geril watched them with his mouth hanging open.

There were more of them than he could count, all of them resembling Thrag. Many wore bracelets around their wrists and ankles that appeared to be silver.

As many more wore spiked helmets of leather and metal. Thrag himself was now clad in thin plate armor and wore what looked to be gem encrusted silver bracelets on each arm. His friend gestured to a distant opening. "Hee waaaits," he said.

"Who waits, Thrag?"

Thrag answered by stepping behind Geril and lifting him. The great wings unfolded as he stepped over the edge and took to the air. They glided through the multitude of flying figures, Geril wincing each time it seemed they would collide. Thrag flew without hesitation, sometimes barking a greeting to others they passed. Geril risked a glance down and shuddered.

The cave floor was far below and all but hidden by a swirling mist through which scores of frostwings cavorted. The mist did not hide the myriad of thick stalagmites that covered the floor. A fall from this height… He gulped and quickly looked up again.

They reached the opening Thrag had pointed out. The mighty wings beat harder as he prepared to land on the narrow ledge, his powerful legs taking the shock of impact. Geril was lowered gently to the rock. The entrance to this new cave was much larger than the one to the cave he had slept in. Thrag would not even have to lower his head to enter.

Two frostwings crouched on either side. Both wore the silver bracelets he had seen on others of their kind, but neither wore the thick ankle bands. To his surprise, both held weapons. One of them gripped the hilt of a short sword, and the other clutched the long handle of a battle-axe twice the size of Geril's. They looked at Geril with open curiosity and not, he was pleased to see, the slightest trace of malice. A hard talon nudged Geril from behind, guiding him into the cave.

It was a room rivaling the council chamber of Balgavarr in size. The walls and ceiling were coated with more of the mirrored ice, making the chamber bright. But the light also reflected off of piles of precious gemstones and metal. Geril gaped. This was a treasure far more vast than the riches of Balgavarr. If the morehl ever learned of this, even the cold would not daunt them. The room was also filled with weapons of all types. Swords, axes, maces, crossbows, and bows of all sizes lay in heaps or leaned against the rock walls.

The vaghan warrior stood aghast. With what was in this single room, he could equip every soul in Balgavarr. There were enough implements of war to supply a grand army. Even the selumari did not possess such a store. He glanced up at Thrag as he lifted a sword to examine it. To his astonishment, he saw the morehl symbol for the rakshasa etched into the slender blade.

That alone marked the poniard as a family emblem. The morehl held such weapons in high regard, going so far as to retrieve such a blade from the hands of a fallen comrade on the field of battle. Setting it back down, he noticed other makes of swords in the group. He identified the curved cutlasses of the selumari, and the unusual kukri of the amazons. Next to the swords lay a pile of axes. He saw both the crude and efficient stone hatchets of the trogs, and the more deadly creations of his own race. Turning to Thrag he asked, "How did your people come to possess these weapons?"

A thick and growling voice spoke from behind him. "The races of the lowlands have always littered the earth with such things after battle. We simply clean up the mess."

Geril turned and stumbled back into Thrag with surprise. The creature that stood before him was not one of the frostwings, as he had expected to find. Instead, he faced a creature that his people had thought long gone from the region. One of the feral folk.

The feral were one of the younger races of Esfah. In the old tongue of the ancients they were named the ghwereste, meaning "ones from animals."

As war had ravaged the face of Esfah, Nature called forth a new breed that would battle for the preservation of life. Turning to the beasts of the earth and air, she granted them intelligence, power, and size enough to become her champions. Where the sky met the land they thrived, boasting great courage and ferocity, but tempered with wisdom and compassion. They were full of wild and barbarous vitality, the primal force of Nature brought to savage life.

Something about this one spoke to Geril, and he suspected him to be a shaman of the race by his markings and the staff he carried. The wolverine was taller than the dwarf but far shorter than Thrag. It was clothed in a long robe that covered it almost entirely, leaving only the clawed hands and head exposed.

It held a length of golden ironwood in one hand. The rod was covered with runes, and the top had been carved into the shape of a flying dragon. The shaman leaned on the staff wearily. "I am Caulte. You are Geril son of Ghuren, of the vagha. You are welcome here."

"Where is here?"

Caulte took him by the arm and led him back to the opening of the cave. He gestured with the staff. "The frostwings have no real name for this land of ice. But if it were to be named, it would be called Icehome. Here they have thrived for years, unknown to the races until you discovered your friend Thrag."

"How did you come to be among them? None of the vagha has seen any of the feral for several generations. We thought your race dead."

Caulte lowered his head. "As it almost was. The armies of Death have ravaged this world, but this you know. Your people have fought the morehl for many years, as have mine. You know my race. This itself is a surprise. We believed for too long that the elder races had forgotten us. For many years we fought Death's agents, and always we prevailed so long as we did not leave the golden plains of Seshara."

Geril gasped. *Seshara! By the fire of Eldurim, the homeland of the amazons.*

Caulte nodded. "I see by your face you know the name. Yes, we fought side by side with the amazons. Together we held back the hordes of Death and celebrated each victory. The humans were valiant allies."

"What happened to them? We sent messengers there. They promised us their help. Then they were gone. We never knew what happened."

Caulte thumped the heel of his staff on the floor. A shower of sparks flew up around the shaman as his eyes grew cold. "A betrayal, friend dwarf. A vile betrayal. The amazon war chief Jossin and his army came to us. He spoke of the dwarves and the coral elves. He told us that it would please *Tarvanehl, Who Is All,* for them to help you against the morehl. Although we did not share their belief, we accepted his words. Though the feral crave peace, we delight in battle. It was decided that we would accompany them.

"Then came one of the selumari, who spoke that the threat was gone. The morehl had gone, and our assistance was no longer needed. We put away our weapons and allowed our battlelust to cool. The amazons camped within the borders of our lands as they prepared to return to their city. Under the cover of night, the morehl attacked. Caught unready, both of our armies were decimated."

"Decimated?" Geril was dumbfounded. How could the morehl have defeated the armies of both the amazon and the feral? The lava elves had never been that strong, even with the trogs aiding them. "What happened?"

"The morehl that attacked us fought not just with the goblins. They brought with them four legions of the undead."

Geril gasped. The undead were other creatures of the Shadowlands. There were rumors that the dead sometimes wandered across the icy tundra; his father had said as much—they'd begun to rise in small groups in the days after the sacrifice of Zephras "Thunderfist," but few credible tales existed.

During a time of Nature's greatest despair over the ravaging of Esfah, Death had risen on wings of blackness and swept across the world. In its wake, the dead stirred. All manner of corrupt forms rose from their graves or emerged from dank holes in the earth. Skeletons, zombies, wraiths, ghouls, and worse marched against the cities of the living. A hideous new era of war had fallen upon Esfah. Many believed that Death would finally triumph. Even the morehl had lost countless numbers to the terrifying swarm of decay. For the lava elves to be allied with the legion was too appalling to dwell on.

Caulte squatted down until his eyes were level with Geril's. "The undead fell upon us like a dark shadow. Our soldiers were overcome by wights and zombies, while the amazons lost hundreds to skeletons and revenants led by a death knight. I lost many of my apprentices to a lich before I was able to cast a helpful spell. The lich was torn apart by its own troops. Once it was gone, I realized that both armies had been under a spell it had cast. By then it was too late. We had lost far too many. Our lead hunter was gone. It fell to me to lead. I chose to retreat. Many of my people despised me for it, but it let us survive."

"You had no choice," Geril sympathized. "So that is why our runners found the amazon city deserted. They fled Seshara as you did."

"I cannot believe that they were exterminated. Tarvanehl would never allow his children to be destroyed. The amazon nursed their wounds as we did. They will return to Seshara from wherever they have gone, as we will." The wolverine pointed with the staff toward the open space of the vast cavern and the swooping forms within it. "The frostwings discovered us when we crossed into the Shadowlands. Weakened as we were, we prepared to fight one last time. We never expected to find mercy at the hands of such creatures. They brought us here, and here we have healed. Here we have prepared for our return to the plains of Seshara."

A sudden horrifying thought occurred to Geril. Anger rose up in him and the words spilled from his lips before he could think to stop them. "With the frostwings helping you? What of my people? The morehl already invade our lands in search of Balgavarr!" He regretted the words the moment they were spoken. He slapped his hand over his mouth and lowered his head. "I always speak before thinking," he said, words muffled behind his fingers.

"A failing of youth, and one easily forgiven. I understand your concern for your people, but the frostwings refused when we asked for their help."

"Refused?" Geril felt his hope fades. He leaned against the hard rock of the cavern. "Refused."

Caulte nodded while he scratched behind one ear with the wingtip of the carved dragon on his staff. "They feared that Death would find them and punish them. They venture out of the Shadowlands only rarely and in few numbers. Thrag was hunting when he was shot by the morehl."

"So my trip here was wasted." Geril looked around for Thrag. The frostwing was stretched out full length on the floor, idly picking his teeth with one long talon. "Take me home, Thrag."

Caulte stepped between him and Thrag. "The frostwings would not fight with us, but they will fight with you."

The words stunned the dwarf. "What?"

"The frostwings had no reason to join with us. Nothing to compel them to battle. But you saved the life of one of their own, and they see the honor of that deed. By the command of their leader, they will leave the only home they have ever known, and travel to Balgavarr."

"When can I see their leader and give him my thanks?"

Caulte panted, a sound Geril recognized as laughter. "You already have. While the frostwings have no care or knowledge for what the Elder Races call royalty, you may consider Thrag the areosan king. As the greatest of their warriors, they follow his commands."

Geril stared at Thrag. "Their king? I… don't know… what purpose do you serve here?"

"To repay our debt to them, I act as Thrag's interpreter whenever they have dealings with lowlanders. This is the first time. You saved Thrag's life. They are indebted to you."

Thrag sat up and grinned in his sharp-toothed way. He seemed to be laughing.

"That is not all, friend dwarf. Our paths lie together. My people will come as well. The ghwereste seek revenge for the loss we suffered. We will join the battle. We will fight, and together we will drive the morehl back to their home among the fiery peaks."

"The feral will come? How many of you are there?"

"I will show you." Geril's arm was taken in a gentle but firm grasp.

Caulte leaned heavily on his staff as he led the dwarf back into the weapons cavern and through it. They went through a smaller opening and into another vast cave. Geril blinked at the differences he saw. The frostwings lived among the rough-hewn crags of cold rock and ice. In this cave there was warmth from both the sunlight streaming in through the opening in the ceiling and the numerous fires across the cavern floor. Straw covered the floor, as did the Gherweste. Their numbers were even greater than the frostwings. The dwarf didn't even try to count them. The cave was filled with sparring warriors, their weapons clashing and filling the cavern with echoes. Females and young slept or watched the mock battles from scattered nests along the edge of the cavern walls.

Caulte lifted his staff. A ball of fire shot from the tip and lit up the cavern. The feral turned as one to stare at them. Then they roared.

Geril winced at the sound and prepared to flee, but Caulte grabbed his arm and held him firm. "The ghwereste are ready to fight with you, Geril son of Ghuren. Lead us to battle."

Geril stood stunned for a moment, then he grinned and lifted his axe high. "To battle!" he shouted. "To battle!"

The feral mimicked him, lifting their own weapons and taking up the chant.

"To battle! To battle! To battle!"

# PART 3

*"Only when all races bow to the morehl, will we know true victory."*
—*Emperor Saugor, 1020 SA*

Laman frowned at the spy that stood dripping before him. There was a puddle of water on the tent floor beneath the lava elf's feet. The lower caste fighter was no doubt counting every breath he made as if it might be his last.

When summoned before a conqueror, one could expect either punishment or reward. Punishment was usually painful, and more often fatal, and Laman was not known for his rewards. It was a reputation he relished. He picked up the pistol lying on the table next to his chair, suppressing a smile at the barely heard intake of breath a few feet away.

"Why has your caste failed me?" he asked quietly. "Why do the vagha remain undiscovered?" He toyed with the pistol. It was not his weapon of choice, but he knew enough to operate it. The spy knew this as well.

Bowing his head as a sign of respect he said, "Milord, we search diligently. Balgavarr is well hidden." The spy's eyes never left the pistol.

"Aye, this I know. We expect the vagha to be clever, do we not? Are not both of our races born of Firiel's fire?"

"They have magic, milord. We think they use it to make the ground hide them, and their movements."

Laman put the pistol down again and stood up. "You think? I do not care for guesses or suppositions. You were placed in charge when Amos was killed. You swore to me at Tulgesh that I would not be wrong to place my confidence in you and your forces. Have I erred, Egan? Was I foolish to place so much faith in an underling just because of who his father was?"

"Milord, we need but a little more time…" Egan began, but his words were cut off when the sword tip touched the base of his throat. He'd not even seen Laman draw the powerful weapon. A vorpal sword in any warrior's hands was bad enough; in the hands of a conqueror it was frightening.

"Time?" Laman shouted. "You have had more time than you deserve! Amos would have found the dwarves by now! You dishonor his name by your very presence," he spat. "Three days we have waited while you and your group have searched. I give you only one more. Fail me again, and you will join your father groveling at the feet of Lord Death. Now go."

Egan bowed and ducked quickly through the tent flaps. Outside, thunder rumbled as an unseasonal rain poured down. Laman smirked at the retreat of the underling. The pistol was not even loaded, but it served as an effective tool of intimidation.

Abruptly he sighed in both disgust and irritation. He hated this region of Esfah. His own homelands were higher and hotter. Rain fell infrequently and then only in short bursts that raised clouds of steam from the hot ground.

The peaks where the morehl made their homes were also free of this thrice-cursed plant life. There the trees were scraggly and few. Here in the land of the vagha there were trees everywhere, making it easier for the enemy to remain hidden, or to conceal them before an attack. His soldiers were jumpy, seeing dwarves behind every limb and leaf. Every passing day it became more difficult to maintain his control.

He slumped onto his cot with a heavy sigh. With a snarl he opened the small brazier that glowed near the cot and placed more twigs on the low flames.

Would it never grow warm in this blasted land? Just one more thing to add to his growing list of frustrations. Since they had found the remains of the last patrol into this region, his soldiers had considered this land haunted by unknown and hideous creatures. The damage done to the patrol had been horrifying.

The dwarves were known to have control over some powerful creatures like the roc, umber hulk, and androsphinx. He had seen soldiers wounded and killed by such things, but what they had found this time was entirely new. His men had been literally torn apart with such force that the blood had splattered for several paces in all directions. The duelist in charge of the scouting party had been missing both arms, and what was left of him looked to have fallen from a great height. He had seen fall victims before; such things were unavoidable for a race that dwelt among the high crags. But where could the duelist have fallen from? There were no cliffs high enough in the area.

It was unfortunate that those who found the bodies had been too ignorant to keep the discovery to themselves. Word had spread as rapidly as hot lava down a hill, demoralizing the troops even more. He could feel the dissent gaining strength in the camp. If the dwarves were not found soon, he could very well find himself at their mercy. This was the only thing about this campaign that caused him to feel fear.

One did not become a conqueror without having faced fear and beaten it down. In his youth he had killed a roc single-handedly, saving the life of his commander and earning himself a rapid promotion. Though wounded terribly, he had found later that little frightened him anymore. Even the sight of a coral giant off the coast of Tulgesh had only aroused curiosity about the creature's abilities and strength. He had led the charge that had brought the giant crashing down. That victory was easily attributed to the well-placed shots of the assassins, but it was to him they cheered as the water lapped against the huge corpse.

His eyes went wide. Of course! The morehl followed where he led. He could not sit here and wait for the vagha to be handed to him on a silver tray.

If the dwarves were to be found, he would have to find them. He buckled on his sword belt as he got to his feet. The sword hissed as it was sheathed. He had sworn to Emperor Saugor that both Tulgesh and Balgavarr Reaches would be taken. The sword had been the King's gift to him for making that promise. He would see that vow through.

Throwing his cape around his shoulders, he cursed the rain again as he left the tent.

The sun was setting as he walked through the camp. He ignored the soldiers crouched around their fires. His eyes, however, saw their thinly disguised looks of contempt and inquietude. Many blamed him for the failure to take Balgavarr and made no secret of it. He had ferreted out many of the malcontents, but execute one for treason and two more took their place. If Balgavarr was not found and taken soon, even the sword he carried would not be enough to save him from a mob determined to see him dead.

Within moments he left the camp and entered the wooded hills. The rain was starting to taper off, but a mist was rising in its place. The temperature was dropping quickly, and he wrapped his long cape tighter around himself and shivered. He would make this a short excursion; to stay out in this cold too long could result in disaster. Lava elves could not survive long without heat. These cold mountains seemed to leech the warmth from his very bones. Soon his teeth were chattering.

For an hour he stumbled over roots and rocks that seemed to spring up from the earth to daunt him. How could the dwarves abide such a place? For the first time he questioned the wisdom of Saugor in his desire to possess such a land, even if it was rich with gold and precious stones. The understood the plains of Seshara. The rich soil of the lush grasslands was perfect for farming and hunting. He smiled despite the chill. That had been a glorious battle. The feral and the amazons together had nearly driven back the morehl from the plains, but neither had counted on the undead. That had turned the tide.

Even now the legion waited for his call. Many of the soldiers had been uneasy about joining with the legion. The undead had their own agenda, and what they did with the bodies of slain enemies was unspeakable. Still, they fought with an unmatched ferocity that had caused even the conflict-loving feral to flee. He chuckled. It was either that, or the stench they made. A platoon of zombies and ghouls was not exactly pleasing to the nose. The animal-like feral were more sensitive to such smells than their human allies, and were promptly routed, despite their racial hatred for the undead.

The warrior women of the amazons had fought on as their hairy comrades fled the battlefield. Blood had stained the golden plains of Seshara.

The thick grass had been trampled flat for miles, and the blood had mixed with the earth to make a rancid mud that the undead delighted in. The lich that had led the magical troops had cast numerous spells, causing the dead of all the armies to rise and fight against their former comrades. Laman had been nearby, directing the movement of the troops. He'd heard the lich preparing to cast a hindering spell, but before it could finish the amazon oracle had used her magic to summon a great wall of fog that effectively obscured their retreat. The amazon city of Thurisa had been abandoned before the morehl arrived. Where they had gone remained a mystery.

Seven years later, he and his troops were sent from Seshara to Tulgesh.

The coastlands were rich in mineral wealth, necessary for the production of the powder used in pistols. The undead had declined to join that combat and returned to whatever land they called home. Matrek's forces had been prepared. Their scouts had ventured far from the coastal city and had seen the dust cloud of the morehl army as it marched toward them. They had even had time to send a plea for help to the damned vagha. The dwarves had come almost at once. Laman had been counting on the fact that relations between the dwarves and the coral elves had been almost non-existent for many years.

After a long battle, the selumari city was now theirs. The majority of the morehl forces remained there to maintain control of the few selumari that had been captured when the city fell. The coral elf captives had been put to work immediately, securing much needed supplies for the troops and showing the location of rich treasures that were hidden away. The uncooperative ones were quickly executed, making the rest more than happy to do as they were told.

Only one vagha had been captured. A too-proud wizard named… Latkis. Yes, that was it. The old fool had been waiting for them behind the sealed door that led to the council chamber of Tulgesh. As soon as the door had been forced, hundreds of dancing lights had surrounded the invaders. A simple spell known to the magic users of the morehl, but still effective when cast properly. Laman watched as his soldiers ran around in confusion, then he strode through the colorful display and placed his sword against the wizard's neck. "Stop at once," he had said calmly, "or die."

The wizard had been no fool. The lights winked out at once, and the old dwarf was quickly chained and dragged away. Laman had no idea if the dwarf was still alive or not. He had wanted to attend the interrogation, but had been sent to the Kafnysan Mountains to track down the home of the vagha. During his absence, his soldiers were demolishing the city, searching for what they thought was treasure, but was instead what Laman knew to be the key to total victory in Cyrea.

Now here he was, tripping through the darkness in a strange and uncomfortable land. Another root seemed to reach out and grab his ankle.

Only a last-second grab at the trunk kept him from falling. He remembered stories from his childhood of an ancient and powerful race of sentient trees that had fought his kind for generations. It was only a myth, but in the dark among the trees, such stories had a way of seeming real. Soon every branch would appear to be grabbing for him if he dwelled on such things.

Frustrated at his failure to find anything, he had just decided to turn back when he heard voices. Crouching down behind the nearest large boulder, he froze.

Two dwarves were creeping through the underbrush. Their steps were slow and nearly silent as they moved. They stopped only a few steps away. "I thought I saw something, Hergat," one of them said.

"You're always jumping at shadows, Jeffon. It's far too cold for any morehl to be out."

Jeffon frowned and stared hard at the boulder where Laman crouched.

The lava elf knew that the top of his head was visible as he watched them. If he moved, he would give himself away. In the darkness, they would mistake it as just a part of the rock. Grateful for his dusky red complexion, he tried to refrain from even blinking.

"I could swear something moved by that rock." His hands tightened on the haft of the axe he carried.

His companion took him by the arm. "Enough already, Jeffon. Let's get back. I need a warm fire and a cold ale." The two moved off and Laman sighed in relief. Not that he feared battling two dwarves, for his sword would have been more than a match for both of them.

Just the thought of battle caused the sword to vibrate on his hip. It lusted for blood and battle, just as Laman did. Almost he started to draw it out, but then reconsidered. Instead of attacking the dwarves, perhaps it would be better to follow them. There was only one vaghan city in these mountains.

They could only have come from there. Thus decided, he started after them.

Elder Vors watched as the doors to the tunnel slowly opened. The massive rock portal made only a soft grating sound as the two halves separated. Concern etched his craggy features as the scouts entered. They had been on patrol for several hours, much longer than they had planned on being gone. Many had grown concerned at their extended absence. They approached with heads bowed. "Elder," they said together.

"Did you see anything?"

"Nothing," Jeffon said. "I thought I saw something, but it was probably just an animal."

Vors sighed heavily in relief. "Nothing of the morehl?"

"It is as Jeffon said, Elder. We saw nothing except shadows."

A voice spoke from behind Vors. "The agents of Death know the shadows. Within them they become invisible. They use them to move unseen." Ghuren stepped into view. "Do not discount what Jeffon saw, young Hergat. I believe the morehl are near."

"None of them have ever been seen at these heights," Vors scoffed.

"They despise the cold night winds. I believed your son when he told us of his encounter with a scouting party. I suspect it was nothing more than that. We will see no more of the morehl."

"Such confidence is ultimately disastrous. Where one scouting party is known there are at least three more that go unseen. The morehl are not to be dismissed so lightly."

Vors crossed his arms and tried to look at his old rival without letting the contempt he felt show on his face. "The morehl would have attacked by now if they knew where we were."

Ghuren shook his head. "How quickly things change with you, Vors. Is it so easy to dismiss the obvious? The morehl are here. They will find us, and they will attack us, and our city will fall to their superior numbers."

Vors sneered. "We are the children of Eldurim, He would never allow the lava elves to conquer us." The two footmen looked at each other with growing discomfort. Cautiously they backed away from the two arguing leaders of the city and made their escape.

"Eldurim and Firiel may have made us, but they leave us to determine our own destinies. We will be found, and Eldurim will not interfere. If we survive, we will honor him. If we pass from Esfah, he will turn his eyes to other communities of vagha."

"You believe we will fall? Do you have so little faith in our warriors?"

Ghuren turned away and stared out into the night. A fresh breeze found its way through the portal and caressed his face with its cool touch. The rain had stopped, and stars were winking in the clearing sky. His old body ached with age, and he wondered if he would live through another day to see them shine again. "I have faith that they will fight until the last of them falls. How can I doubt them? Their very homes and families are at stake." He looked back over his shoulder at his old friend. "Pray my son returns with the frostwings. I believe them to be our only hope." He faced the night again.

Moving as quickly as his tired joints would allow, he walked through the doors and into the darkness.

The guards watched him leave, then turned to Vors. "Elder? Should someone go with him?"

Vors shook his head. "Of all the people in this city, he is perhaps the one who knows this mountain better than any other. No harm will befall him. Keep the doors open until he returns, but double the guard. We will listen to his words and take no chances." He watched the darkness for a moment more, then turned away. "There are no morehl," he whispered. "He will be safe." The words sounded hollow, and he said them again. But no matter how many times he said them, he was unable to believe them.

Laman stared at the open doors to Balgavarr. He could not believe his luck. He'd set out to find the city and had done just that. His camp was practically on top of it! While anxious to take the city, he was not so foolish as to rush into a group of heavily armed dwarves. He would have all the soldiers he needed as soon as he took word back to Tulgesh. A wyvern rider could have him there in a day. A few days to prepare, then a hard tenday march for the army to arrive. He could be patient that long.

He watched as the scouts conferred with two older dwarves, but he was too far away to make out any words. Then one of the old ones walked out of the city. The vagha moved slowly, his steps taking him closer to the place where Laman crouched in his hiding place. This was an unexpected turn of events, and a fortunate one. The dwarf could provide valuable information about the city's defenses. He waited until the dwarf had passed him, then took a last look at the entrance to Balgavarr. Tomorrow the downfall of the city would begin and all of its treasures would be his. He forced down his excitement and moved silently after the vaghan.

Despite the apparent age of his prey, the dwarf moved with ease and surefootedness of one that knew his surroundings well. The terrain grew increasingly rocky the further they moved from the city. Laman found it more and more difficult to move without a sound. This was going to make capturing the dwarf complicated.

They were at least a league from the city when the vaghan stopped.

Surrounded by a grove of tall pines, he sat wearily upon a stump and leaned heavily on his walking staff. "You move well, my friend," he said. "Almost I did not notice you."

Laman's hand went instinctively to the hilt of his sword. Then he relaxed. Even without the vorpal sword, he was strong enough to best the old dwarf. But how had he given himself away? He decided against revealing himself too soon. "You surprise me, old one. I must be getting careless as I grow older. When did you hear me?"

Ghuren chuckled. "Heard you? My hearing was never so good. I never heard a thing. The breeze gave me your scent. You were upwind from me ever since we left Balgavarr. The morehl have a particular smell. Your kind should really get over their aversion to water and bathe now and again." The chuckle turned into a short laugh. "I guess I just gave away one of our tactical advantages."

Laman cursed under his breath. In the excitement of tracking one of the enemy, he'd given himself away without realizing it. Of all the races of Esfah, only the feral could track by scent better than the vagha. "Clumsy of me to forget about that. It won't happen again."

Ghuren turned toward where he heard the voice. "I imagine it won't. The morehl may be thickheaded, but they are far from stupid. Why don't you come out so we can talk face to face?"

Laman hesitated. He was wary, but what possible danger could there be? He stepped out from behind the tree.

The dwarf smiled at him from behind his thick white beard. "A good evening to you, my friend. How do you like our mountain?"

Laman looked about before shrugging. "If it weren't for the trees and the damned cold, I would think I was home. I don't know how you vagha stand it. You don't even have a heavy cloak on, and I'm near to freezing."

Ghuren motioned to a large rock nearby and waited until the lava elf was seated before speaking. "Another difference in our people. To me this is a balmy summer night. There is a bite to the breeze that my old bones feel, but someone younger would not notice. I think the fire of Firiel does not burn as strongly in the morehl as it does within the vagha."

Laman shook his head in disgust. "I take it that you believe the tales of creation. I never found much use for them myself."

Ghuren's smile was sad. "I have read the *Book of the Land*. Many of the passages within it speak truth about the races. Have you read it?" Laman shook his head. "According to it, the morehl and the vagha are almost related, but distant cousins at best. Most unlearned people think you are kindred to the selumari. That is a common mistake. Our two people are both descended of Firiel."

"Religious nonsense," Laman scoffed. "Elves and dwarves are too different."

"Not as different as you may think. Of course, the morehl also share similarities with the trogs," Ghuren said with a wink.

Laman bristled at the insult but decided to change the subject. Religious matters always made him nervous. "Why are you not afraid? Do you not fear death at my hands?"

Ghuren sat up straighter and sighed. "Fear death? No. Death is but a part of life. I have lived a long time, longer than most warriors of my race. I have been expecting my end for some time, but I do not believe you will kill me."

"Oh? Why is that?" This old dwarf was strange to say the least.

"I pose no threat to you. What purpose would my death serve? You know where the entrance to our city lies, and I am too old to fight you and keep you from telling your soldiers. Besides, you have questions for me. Questions I will not answer."

That much was true. The dwarf was perceptive. Laman leaned forward anyway. "Tell me of your defenses," he said.

"This I will not do. I will not give you an easy victory."

"It could save lives," Laman offered. "Including your own."

"And yours as well," Ghuren countered. "Do you think we will not resist? You may know where we are, but you have yet to gain entry. You do not strike me as the type to send others to fight while he stands back and watches. You may fall just as easily as I."

"How many warriors do you have ready? You sent troops to Tulgesh. How many remain?"

Ghuren smiled. "This entire war is foolish. What do your people need with our home? With Tulgesh or Seshara? Everything you need already exists in your own homeland. What is this madness that drives you to conquer all you consider inferior?"

Laman ignored the words. "What monsters do you command? Tell me of your umber hulks and gargoyles." He drew out his sword and stuck it point first into the ground. Ghuren pretended not to notice.

"The races of Esfah will never willingly be slaves of the morehl. The trogs may be content to live that way, but the rest will not yield more easily than we of Balgavarr. Too soon you will find yourselves masters of none, and the morehl will be exterminated. The forces of Nature will prevail."

Laman growled and stood up. He was angry now, and the cold was not helping matters. The old dwarf was talking nonsense. Perhaps he was senile.

"If I let you live, will you tell your people to surrender?"

"The citizens of Balgavarr would not do so even if I were to ask them, you must know that."

"And you must know that I cannot allow you to return and give warning of our presence." The elf lifted his sword and let the moonlight play along the blade. The light reflected into Ghuren's eyes, making him wince.

"Do to me what you must, but there is one thing I will tell you. If you are wise, and a true leader among your people, you will heed my words."

Laman laid the blade across his shoulder. "Speak," he said. Despite the anger, he was coming to admire the courage of the old dwarf warrior.

"The vagha have been aware of you for some time now. Steps have been taken to make sure that no morehl sets foot within Balgavarr. We are not a people that seek vengeance, but you invade our lands and threaten the lives of our people and the futures of our children. A chill wind comes to cleanse our lands of your evil."

Laman rolled his eyes. "Nothing can save your people," he said. "You can't even save yourself." He brought down the sword and thrust it through the stomach of the dwarf. The sword sang as it drank deeply of an enemy's blood. With ease, he pulled the humming blade from the body of his sworn enemy. Blood gushed from the wound.

Ghuren's eyes were all that showed his pain as he collapsed and fell from the stump. His strength waning, he managed to roll over onto his back.

He would watch the stars as he died. Always he had watched the stars. Perhaps he would wake on another world, or maybe wander this one as a spirit. That would be better. He could watch over his son. His eyes found those of the lava elf. "I pity you," he whispered.

Laman got to one knee to better hear the dwarf's last words. "Why would you pity me? Pity yourself and all of your people that will die when they fight against us."

Ghuren coughed and blood speckled his lips. Pain racked him, but there were words that needed to be spoken. "Your army will never... see the inside of the city. A chill... wind... comes. It will sweep... your army... from our land." With a sigh, he looked to the stars again. "A... chill... wind... comes..." he whispered.

Laman watched as the life faded from the eyes of the vaghan. "Old fool." He stood and wiped the blade clean. What had the dwarf meant by a chill wind? He looked down at the body. There had been no joy in this kill, no honor. The dwarf had been right, his death had served no purpose. In that moment, Laman realized his mistake.

The conqueror slumped to the rock he had sat on while talking. The dwarf had obviously been an Elder. He would be missed. When he failed to return, the city would be alerted. They would be prepared when the army arrived. This had not occurred to him until too late. He slammed his fist against the cold stone. Too late! He had always prided himself on his ability to keep his emotions under stringent control, yet he had allowed an enemy to goad him into an action that could lead to disaster.

He leaped to his feet and slid the sword back into its scabbard before setting off back to his camp. He would leave tonight. There was now no time to delay. Still, the words haunted him. Had the dwarf been speaking of some magical spell when he spoke of a wind? He dismissed the notion immediately. It had only been a last attempt to frighten him. Nothing more. Even if the vagha had some new magic, it would not be enough to keep his army from taking the city.

He started laughing as he thought more about it, and the laughter echoed into the night.

# PART 4

*"Death seeks always to conquer through fear. His minions know not mercy or pity, though they be pitiful themselves."*

*—Alrys Windsinger, The Cyrean Songs 798 SA*

Far to the south of the Kafnysan mountains and near the Shining Sea lay a mostly unexplored and inhospitable region. Here one would see only stunted and twisted trees and brown, withered grasses that struggled for life in the blackened ground. Smoking craters were scattered around puddles of boiling mud and tar that dotted the landscape amid streams of dark, fetid water that bubbled up from the heart of the earth. Tall rock formations stuck up like the fingers of a long-buried giant, the sharp jagged edges stabbing, knifelike, hundreds of feet into the sky.

The trogs saw this land in the distorted visions of their dreams when they danced their dark rites under the full moons. The vagha knew of it but did not speak of it. The selumari, perhaps the most traveled of the races, had seen it from their coral ships, but had never thought to leave the skies and seas to investigate and explore. Even from a great distance, the earth looked deformed and poisonous, defying anything whole and hale to step within its boundaries. Only the lava elves did not fear it, but they had learned to respect the forces they suspected dwelled there. Death had taken this part of the earth and transformed it to an image that pleased him.

In all the years that war had ravaged the face of Esfah, no battles had been fought on this warped soil, for none of the races of Nature believed that anything could survive in such a forbidding and eerie place.

The selumari named this terrain the Plagueland, and the other races accepted the appellation readily.

Yet strangely enough, life endured and even flourished here.

A shadow sped over the torn earth, cast from above by the winged figure that flew with haste through the hazy skies. The creature was thin and gangly with skin the color of boiling lava. The wings that swept back from its shoulders seemed too small and frail to hold such a being aloft, yet its flight was swift as it flapped its wings rapidly. It muttered through uneven fangs as it traveled, and its narrow eyes scanned the horizon while the long, pointed ears turned and twisted in every direction.

Then it uttered a sharp snarl and angled down to the earth in an ungainly glide toward a lone figure that stood amidst the ruin of a fallen spire of rock.

It looked as if it would crash, and the figure backed away, but the creature's wings beat hastily at the last moment, and the long toes sank into the soil. Fetid mud oozed up around the feet of the creature like blood.

The lava elf that waited winced as the black eyes settled upon him. Only by steeling himself did he keep from running. The thing was hideous even by morehl standards. It stared at him over a long nose that twitched. The thick black hair on its brow was pulled back in a tight braid that fell between the wings. It stood nearly as tall as him, and even though it appeared frail, he could see the knots of ropy muscle covering the limbs. This was certainly not a creature to underestimate. "I be Lirk," it said, the voice high and grating. "You be one called Taran, elf?"

"I am."

Lirk spread thin lips in what Taran thought to be a grin. "He waits for words," he hissed.

"What happened to Flik?"

"Flik fall down, go splat," Lirk said with rasping laughter.

The elf swallowed hard. "Tell him that we're close to finding the dwarves. The battle will be soon."

Lirk held up a mace with a long handle. The three long metal prongs on the head burned, but Taran could not see how. "Pleased he will be."

Taran's confidence was growing. Apparently Lirk was not going to hurt him.

"My own commander waits for word as well. Will your army join with ours?"

"Lirk knows not. Only he will say. We come to see fight."

Taran scowled. "What do you mean? Flik said that your people would help us take the dwarf city!"

Lirk scowled and Taran backed away from the hideous features. "Flik no speak for all. We fight when we want, who we want." The creature shambled forward and thrust a long, pointed finger against the morehl's chest. "Maybe we fight. Maybe not. If dwarves win, maybe we fight them. We watch. We see. We decide."

Taran slapped away Lirk's hand, his annoyance with the creature overcoming the fear he felt in its presence. "That's not what was agreed on," he snarled.

Lirk's brows narrowed as it examined its hand. "We change minds," it hissed.

"Changed your minds? We gave your people a king's ransom in gold and jewels because we were promised their help." Taran grasped the hilt of his short sword. "I think you should reconsider."

Lirk's eyes gleamed and it squeezed the handle of the mace until its knuckles cracked loudly. The mysterious flames burned brighter, as if fueled by the anticipation of battle. "You want fight?" it breathed. "I give you fight." It hissed and swung the mace.

Taran ducked and the weapon *whooshed* over his head. He drew his poniard as battle lust flooded through him. He would teach this wretch a lesson. He wouldn't kill it, but it would learn to respect a warrior of the morehl. He threw himself into a somersault toward Lirk and thrust the sword up.

Lirk yelped and jumped back, but not before the tip of the blade punctured its side. Dark red blood jetted from the wound. Taran jumped up and knocked the mace from Lirk's hand with his sword. Lirk howled as the vibration from the impact stung it. The elf wasted no time charging into Lirk and bowling the creature over. For a moment, they rolled in the sour dirt wrapped in Lirk's wings. When they stopped, Taran sat astride the thin chest of the creature he had at first feared. He held his sword to its neck. "My commander told me to step softly with your kind," he panted. "He said we needed you, but he suspected that you would turn against us without warning. How prophetic he was."

Lirk's eyes were wide and darted around as if searching for help. "You pass test, elf," it said.

Taran laughed. "Desperate words that I don't believe. Your kind believes itself superior to mine. Why would you feel the need for a test? I think you at last know what fear is. Should I introduce you to my lord? Shall I send you into the presence of Death?"

Lirk's head shook wildly. "No kill," it rasped. "If dead, no can bring rest to fight."

"So now you agree to fight with us? Why do I feel no truth behind your words? You'll attack me as soon as my back is turned."

Lirk's hands slowly came up in the sign of submission. "I not kill elf," it said. "Elf not kill me. We come help fight."

Taran leaned against the blade, causing the edge to press against the rough skin of the creature under him. A trickle of blood oozed down Lirk's neck.

Any more pressure and he would slit Lirk's throat, and Lirk knew it. "Take this message to your kind," he growled. "If the scalders attack the morehl, we will march into your lands and exterminate every last one of you."

"We will come," Lirk snarled. "but much gold will you need."

"Gold we will have when Balgavarr Reaches is ours. The vagha are a wealthy race. Your payment is assured, so long as you know where your loyalties lie." Slowly he stood, keeping the tip of the sword at Lirk's neck. He backed away as Lirk scrambled to its feet.

The scalder retrieved its mace and stared at Taran with hate-filled eyes. "Be warned, elf. We will come, but morehl never come to Plaguelands again. They die if they do." With a flurry of flapping wings, the scalder took flight.

Taran breathed a heavy sigh of relief. Sheathing his sword, he turned and started jogging north. Far in the distance he could see the warped and blackened shape of the giant aldehn tree that marked the boundaries of the Plaguelands. His wyvern was tied there, waiting the return of its rider. It was a long way home, but he had accomplished his mission and the bargain had been struck. Now nothing would keep the morehl from their destiny.

Balgavarr, like Tulgesh, would soon belong to the morehl. His race would soon dominate over all.

In the shadows of a large outcropping of rock, two eyes that glowed with an unearthly light watched the diminishing figure of the lava elf. A dry chuckle came from the fetid mouth. The lich gathered the black cloak he wore and moved deeper into the Plaguelands. He laughed again. "It is time," he said.

Lifting a gnarled staff of aldehnwood, dark magics swirled the air around him. A foul wind howled around it, and the lich raised his bony arms as if to embrace it. "I move as the night," he whispered as the wind took him.

Silence fell again on the Plaguelands.

Geril watched with growing wonder as the warriors of the feral marched from the caverns of the frostwings. It seemed that their numbers were endless. The open area below the mouth of the cave was rapidly filling with warriors, each brandishing crude but deadly stone knives or flexing razor-sharp claws and talons. The vulture-folk shrieked commands at the hawk- and falcon-folk that swooped and dove among the few scattered clouds.

Everywhere Geril looked he saw more and more of the mighty beast people. It was astonishing to the vaghan that these were creatures of Nature, created to be champions of Life. Also amazing was how rapidly they reproduced, which was another reason why they had agreed to help defend Balgavarr. Caulte had told him that their numbers had increased tenfold since they had found refuge among the frostwings.

The dwarf pulled his cloak closer. He almost missed the heavy leather battle armor he had left at home. It was thick and uncomfortable, but it would have kept him warmer. There was no wind, but the air was cold. During the night it had snowed, coating the few scattered bristlebranches and ironwoods with a blanket of white. The morning sunlight reflected off the snow in a brilliant glare, making even the ruddy golden skin of the dwarf appear pale.

The frostwings and feral, covered in heavy fur, seemed unaffected by the chill.

Caulte spoke softly from behind him. "Impressive, are they not?"

"Indeed," Geril replied. "The morehl will know the meaning of fear when they see this mighty army. I am proud to lead them to Balgavarr."

The wolverine placed his hand on Geril's shoulder. "Your path lies elsewhere," he said. "It is not your place to lead us to your home."

"What? Of course I'm going to show them the way. I need to return as soon as I can."

Caulte pointed to the giant figure of a tiger-folk moving among the troops. "That is Eihwaz, our hunter. Born here, his greatest desire is to see the plains of Seshara returned to our people. The memory of our homeland is strong even in the very young, who have never seen it. For this, and the loss of so many, he seeks vengeance against the morehl. He will lead. I will show the way, for I visited Balgavarr many years ago."

Geril shook his head. "I need to return home," he argued. "My place is there. I do not care if I lead or not, but I am going."

There was a heavy thump from behind the two as Thrag announced his arrival with a growl and a blast of wind from his wings. Caulte growled his own greeting in return, then faced Geril again. The dwarf noticed that Thrag now wore gauntlets of silver around his wrists, and heavy plated armor.

Around his waist was a thick leather belt adorned with inlays of silver and gold. Attached to the belt was a stone axe larger than Geril's own. Thrag now appeared as a true warrior of his race.

"A vision came to me in the night," Caulte said. "You and Thrag have another road to follow," he said. "Your way lies to the south."

Anger flashed through the dwarf and he felt all of his muscles tighten.

"Why would I go south, when Balgavarr is to the west? What is south?"

"Tulgesh, and the coral elves."

He blinked his surprise. "Tulgesh? The morehl captured it. There is nothing for me there. Why?"

"The morehl there will be fewer in number. They control the city, but most of their troops will now march to Balgavarr. The city has been found."

"No," Geril whispered, pain in his eyes.

"I wish it was not so. Still, a greater peril lies in Tulgesh. Deep in the city, and away from the eyes of all, lies a great collection of weapons that should never be used again. Fueled by magic, they could make the morehl unstoppable if they are discovered."

"Why were these weapons not used to defend Tulgesh?"

Caulte shook his head. "Of this I am unsure. However, only a handful know they exist at all. It may also be that it is because they are from a dark time of Esfah, when all the races, even the vagha; made and used such things. The raw power of the clash between Nature and Death was harnessed into fearsome weapons, and these were used in battle with horrifying results. It was called the Magestorm."

"I remember hearing stories about a war of magic. In the end, all the artifacts and magical items were gathered and hidden away, lest they destroy the world."

"A few pieces survive, and can be found. You carry one of them in your pouch."

Geril's hand instinctively went to the small leather bag at his belt. "My sightstone?"

Caulte nodded. "It is a small thing, and not inherently dangerous. It allows you a small use of magic. Others, like my staff, in the wrong hands could do great evil. The menace of the lava elves ceased when the Magestorm ended. Only barely were they defeated, and their magical weapons taken."

"And you believe these weapons to be hidden in Tulgesh? As long as the knowledge of them remains secret, what danger is there?" Geril spoke casually, but the thought of a second Magestorm sunk like a stone into his gut.

"There are those among the morehl that remember and seek these forgotten weapons. You fear for your people now; what if this cache of power is found? Nothing will stand against them."

Geril at last grasped the hidden meanings of the conversation. "You want me to go to Tulgesh and find these weapons?"

"No!" Caulte shook his head wildly to emphasize the word. "You must prevent them from being found. Find them and seal them away forever. The artifacts of the Magestorm must never again be used for war."

Geril sighed. "You ask the impossible. Tulgesh is held by the morehl. How do you propose I make my way to the weapons? Stroll to the gate and ask nicely?"

Sarcasm was lost on the feral shaman. "That I cannot tell you. Still, the deed must be done or all will be lost. You must also find the remnants of the selumari army and seek their aid as well. Eihwaz will lead my people and the frostwings to Balgavarr. With luck, we should arrive about the same time you and Thrag return."

"You believe the selumari will come?"

"The only hope of freeing their home lies in the salvation of Balgavarr. Tell Matrek my words. He will come."

The frostwing warriors had gathered on the icy slopes and watched the gathering of the troops below. More of them circled high above, playfully diving among the winged feral. The air was full of barks, growls, and cries of excitement. In every wild heart beat the lust for revenge and the prospect of at long last returning home. Still more of them were busy passing out the massive stone axes that the frostwings used for close combat. Then he blinked in surprise as he saw the frostwing cavalry, mounted on huge blue-black hounds and wolves that bristled with muscle beneath their sleek silvery coats. Behind them marched a parade of gigantic white bears carrying brawny riders. Geril shuddered, glad that they were on his side.

"Hound, Wolf and Bear-masters," Caulte said. "The stalwart cavalry of this young race. Not even a morehl drider can hope to survive an encounter with a bear-master and his steed."

Geril decided not to let Caulte change the subject. "It seems I am always leaving somewhere," he said softly.

"The weapons of the Magestorm are not the only peril. I fear a greater evil is rising."

"A greater evil than the morehl? What could that possibly be?"

"That remains hidden from my sight. All I sense is danger unlike any other I have ever known, and it is growing. If it continues unabated, it could destroy all of Esfah. Its source lies within Deepmire."

This was troubling, and Geril did not doubt a word of it. Magic-users were a mysterious group, and some were able to see into the future. If Caulte had caught a glimpse of what was yet to be, it might be wise to heed such a warning. Still, he did not want to go. His place was in Balgavarr, not traveling to a land held by the morehl. If he was to die, he wanted to die defending his home, not in the damp and salty land of the selumari.

"When do we leave?" he asked with resignation.

"Now," was the soft reply. "The sooner you leave, the sooner you and Thrag can return. Find the weapons of magic and seal them away forever. Not even the selumari must be tempted by the power they harness, and Matrek will see them as a means for his vengeance."

Geril breathed a heavy sigh. For the sake of all things good, he knew he would go. "And the other? What am I to do about that?"

"Discover it, nothing more. Learn what it is and bring word back to all that fight for Nature. Then we will plan how to confront it." There was a thump as another frostwing landed beside Thrag. The two conversed in low growls and snarls; the newcomer then hopped lightly to tower over Caulte.

The wolverine turned and growled his own greeting. "This is Dagaz. He is one of the greatest of the frostwing assailers. From the air he and his troops will rain icy death upon the morehl. He is also the one that will carry me. He is my friend, much like Thrag is yours." He turned golden eyes upon the young dwarf. "You must not fail," he said. "The lives of many races, not just your own, depend upon it." He placed his clawed hands on Geril's shoulders. "I have faith in you, as do we all. You will succeed, of this I am sure. Now go."

Geril tried to speak another word of protest, but Thrag was behind him and lifting him up before the words could leave his mouth. He knew at once that Caulte had planned just that, and his two final words had been Thrag's signal to begin the journey. *Clever old furball*, he thought with a smile as Dagaz bore the shaman away. The feral were different from the vagha, yet Caulte reminded him of his father, Ghuren.

He looked down at Thrag's hairy face, and the frostwing regarded him with cold black eyes that shone with excitement. "We go?"

Thrag growled, his teeth bared in what Geril now knew to be the frostwing equivalent of a smile.

Geril nodded. "It is time," he said. Grabbing a double handful of coarse black fur, Geril held tight as Thrag vaulted effortlessly skyward. For several moments they circled high above the vast army spread out below them, surveying what Geril considered the last hope of Balgavarr. "Go Thrag," he said.

The king of the frostwings banked to the south. Geril struggled to not become angry as they left Balgavarr even further behind. Ghuren had taught his son to always find the good in every bad situation. *At least it will be warm in Tulgesh.*

Taran sat astride his wyvern as the beast flew him the last leagues to Tulgesh. It had been a long flight and his back ached. The meeting with the scalder had not gone as planned, but the outcome would be enough to satisfy Emperor Saugor. Another ally in the war against Nature's forces would be welcomed, but watched carefully. It was the destiny of the morehl to rule all of Esfah, and that included the scalders. They would be put in their place once Balgavarr was taken.

The creatures had been an accidental discovery by a patrol sent to the Plaguelands to look for anything that might aid in the war. That a new race would be found had not occurred to anyone, yet all had seen the possibilities the scalders represented. The necromancers had consulted their dark ways and had seen the hand of Death in the making of the new race. The imps would make formidable allies if they could be swayed to join with the lava elves.

Envoys had been sent, offers made, and at last he had been sent to finalize the bargain. He returned now with news that the scalders would fight alongside the morehl, but at most it would be a fragile alliance. He knew that at some point the imps would betray them. When that would be he did not know, but he was certain of his suspicions. That report would not be received well.

The wyvern skimmed low over the treetops as Tulgesh came into view.

The selumari city, now in the hands of the morehl, was built on the edge of a natural cove. A few coral ships floated on the waves, the rest were scattered wreckage across the floor of the harbor. Captured selumari slaves worked under the hard gaze of morehl taskmasters to restore the few ships that remained. None of them dared turn their eyes upwards as the shadow of the wyvern and its rider passed over them. A few of his kind raised hands in greeting. He ignored them. Most were lower caste, and therefore beneath his notice.

Taran guided his mount toward a distant spire near mid-city. A former temple of Ailuril, it was now the aerie of the wyvern riders. The streets below were filled with lava elves in the act of searching the city for resistance fighters and loot. A few scattered members of the selumari and vagha were also visible, but they were in shackles. The trog fighters were camped in the bogs just outside the city.

His mount angled toward the courtyard where other wyverns and their riders prepared for the coming trip to Balgavarr and the battle. The beast landed with a *thump* and a cloud of dust. It shook its long snout and snorted.

Long wings folded against the body and the beast snarled as a coral elf slave trotted over to it with a large bowl of raw meat. Taran wondered idly what kind of meat it was, then reconsidered. Some things he didn't want to know, especially since there were so many available slaves.

The courtyard of the temple had once been a place of beauty and faith, with marble statues of the selumari gods Ailuril and Aguarehl lined up at intervals along the walls. Now those graven images lay shattered in piles of misshapen rubble. No coral elf image would be tolerated during this occupation. When the morehl had stripped this city of everything of value, it would be abandoned. The selumari survivors hiding in the swamps and forests around Tulgesh would be hunted down and exterminated. The empty city would remain as a silent monument to the race that had built it until the elements reclaimed it.

He tethered the reins to a ring set into one of the stone columns of the temple and made his way inside.

The ironwood doors were smashed and broken, the hinges warped and disfigured. In this place the last of the selumari resistance had taken final refuge. Here they had fallen. Dried pools and splatters of green blood were everywhere, along with a few dark smudges of trog blood. The bodies had been removed and buried in a common grave dug by slaves outside the city, but the gore remained.

He walked through the grand hall, no longer impressed by the large open space and the few pieces of artwork that still hung on the walls. What remained had been defaced with rank smears of muck, but left where they were. The air of the sanctum was thick with the smell of dung from the tall pile of filth that had been heaped around the altar. No morehl would sleep inside this place, so where better to have the slaves take what they shoveled from the courtyard? He did pause briefly to stare at the hideous doorway that haunted his dreams. The steps beyond it descended to the catacombs beneath the temple. But that bothered him little. Morehl were used to subterranean passages. It was the doorway that troubled him. The stones set around it had the appearance of teeth, and the two windows above were shaped like eyes, the glass in them colored blue and green. Walking through that opening made him feel as if he was being swallowed. He shuddered and moved away.

Behind the altar, he entered through a door and ascended the stairs of the tower until he reached another broken door. Inside the large room were a simple table and a single chair, now occupied by Bueron, Captain of this squad of wyvern riders. The commander was clad in the heavy black armor of the morehl, unusual when there was no ongoing battle. His red silken cloak of command, poniard and pistol holster hung on a peg behind him on the wall.

Taran placed his fist to his chest armor in salute and froze until his commander noticed him. Bueron lifted his hand and waved his permission for his underling to relax, but remained focused on the scroll he was reading.

"What news?" he asked.

"The scalders will come, milord, but I fear they will turn on us at the first opportunity."

"This we also suspected. Did the creature attack you?"

"It did, to its regret."

Bueron almost smiled. "Well done. They may fear us now. I knew you were the right one to send. When will they arrive?"

Taran shrugged. "Lirk said they would be there for the battle with the vagha."

The commander nodded almost absently. "Is there more?"

"It gave me a warning to pass on to Emperor Saugor."

Bueron cocked an eyebrow. "Indeed? What is this warning?"

"The morehl are never again to enter the Plaguelands, on pain of death."

"Really? How amusing. I'm certain this news will cause Laman to quake in his boots."

Taran blinked, trying not to show his surprise. "The conqueror has returned to Tulgesh?"

"Only this morning by rider. Balgavarr has been found. The army leaves at sunrise in two days. Our squad has volunteered to lead the riders in the attack against the city."

Eagerness rose in Taran. At long last the vaghan city would be theirs, and the morehl would rule this part of Esfah. Could the rest of the world be far behind? "We will lead them to victory," he said.

"Let us hope so," said a voice from behind him.

Taran spun around. Laman stood in the doorway, idly leaning on the frame. "We must not become so confident that we underestimate the abilities of our enemies. This has led to ruin before. The vagha are staunch defenders of Nature, as powerful as the selumari."

Taran bowed. "Of course not, milord, I meant nothing…"

Laman dismissed the rider with a shrug. "I know what you meant. To see such enthusiasm fuels my own." The conqueror stepped into the room. "I heard what you said about the scalders," he said. "I know our alliance to be a fragile one, perhaps even more so than our truce with the undead. We will watch them closely."

"Rumor says that we owe the discovery of Balgavarr to you, Lord Laman. The Emperor and his Council will surely reward you," Bueron cooed. Taran remained quiet, uncomfortable with the commander's use of such saccharine words in order to curry favor.

Laman seemed not to notice. "Indeed," he replied. "This they have already done. I will lead our forces in the battle against the vagha. When they are mastered, I have been chosen to govern Balgavarr in the name of the Emperor."

Bueron clapped his hands together. "That is good to hear. With you leading us, the dwarves do not stand a chance. The battle will be short, I think."

Laman smirked. "Perhaps. Ready your troops. I will review the wyverns, scorpions, and spiders just before sunset. All must be ready, and I will tolerate no mistakes. Is this understood?" His hand touched the hilt of his sword.

Bueron nodded fiercely. "It is, milord. All will be prepared for your inspection. You will be pleased, I assure you."

Laman lifted his chin and stared down his nose at the commander. His coal-black eyes were hard. "I sincerely hope so, for your sake." Then he turned and left the room.

Bueron slumped into his chair. "That was a veiled threat if I ever heard one." He ran his hand through his short-cropped black hair in frustration. He looked at Taran. "You heard what he said. Go make sure the wyvern riders are ready. I will see to the scorpions and spiders myself. Time is short; only a few hours remain before sunset. I will not find myself at Laman's mercy, Taran. Is that clear?"

"Yes, commander. My riders will not cause you disgrace." He saluted and left the room before Bueron could see the contempt in his eyes. His commander had received a threat and then passed it on. It was the way of the upper ranks, he supposed. Still, if Bueron was demoted it left only one rider to take his place. *My time will come*, Taran smiled to himself. The battle at Balgavarr would secure his own rise to power and wealth. It was a certainty that a squad of wyverns would remain at Balgavarr. Laman would need a good commander, and Taran knew just the elf for the post. In time of war, unfortunate accidents happened to people, and Bueron might fly into someone's pistol sights.

If it didn't just happen, it could be arranged. Fate sometimes needed a nudge in the right direction. Making his plans, the rider made his way down the stairs.

Pauk slogged through knee-deep water. The trog's battle-axe dragged through the water behind him. For almost four days he had been making his way back to Tulgesh after scouting the swamplands that the selumari called Deepmire. He was tired, hungry and in a bad temper. He'd lost his pack of provisions, and then his knife when the crude spear he had made with it had missed the fish and plunged into a particularly deep pool.

To make things even worse, something had eaten his wardog. One moment he'd been jumping for some funny shaped fruit on a high tree branch, his dog idly scratching its ear behind him. Then there had been a splash and a yelp.

When he had turned around, his dog was gone. He was a very unhappy trog when he realized he was going to have to walk back to Tulgesh.

The marshes lay two days from the city and were almost completely unexplored due to the sheer amount of territory they covered. The red elf leader had sent him here with orders to "look around." He had no idea what he was supposed to look for, and he had not found anything except a big something that liked to eat dogs. Usually at home in the swamps, he was anxious to get back to his own troops. Deepmire was nothing like his own homeland of Big Wet, and it scared him. He heard things at night that kept him awake, and food was scarce. He'd gotten lucky that morning, turning over a log and finding a large nest of big white grubs. He had gorged himself and then tucked a few away for later. Later had come and gone and he was hungry again, and the memory of those wonderful grubs made his belly growl. He kept a close watch out for more of those logs.

Hours later, he took a short rest by the side of a large pond of brackish water. Leaning against a tree, he closed his eyes and thought about how much he hated all elves, blue and red. Then something moved in the trees across the pond.

His eyes jerked open and he fumbled for his axe. When he couldn't find it, he scrambled to his feet in panic. He looked around wildly. It had been lying right next to him when he sat down, now it was nowhere to be seen.

Pauk was brave even by goblin standards, but now he was alone and weaponless in a strange swamp. More movement around him, and now he could hear the same sounds that had kept him awake at night, only louder and closer. Hisses and moans surrounded him, and now he could make out words as well. *No weapon – take him – make him ours.* Those words did more to frighten him than the noises. He ran.

More than ever, he missed his dog. He could hear crashes behind him, and shadowy shapes passed him on either side, weaving among the thin tree trunks just out of his sight. Crazed with fear, he missed his footing and tripped over a low branch, falling face first into a shallow pool.

Shadows moved out of the trees and he turned over onto his back.

Long, sinewy figures encircled him. His eyes bulged when he saw what they were. "Let me g-g-go," he moaned, weak with terror. Something darted in from the side and sank long fangs into his arm, tearing open a ragged wound.

He shrieked when he saw it was a snake.

"Bring us the waterssss," a voice called and another of the snake-like creatures produced a flask that they splashed into the wound.

Pauk struggled and one of the fiends insisted, "It must get into his blood."

"We welcome you with the waters of Lethial," another hissed, pouring it directly onto the fangs' puncture wounds.

He struggled a few moments longer, and then a feeling of calm filled him and he lay back. He watched with curiosity as a cool green glow covered his body. With detached interest he regarded his legs as they seemed to fuse together and grow longer. His skin tingled like it did when bugs crawled on it. He was no longer scared and welcomed the shifting of his bones as they moved and twisted inside him.

There was little pain, and it felt like he was growing stronger. Pauk lost sense of time and couldn't say how much of it had passed. He scratched where it itched and his skin sloughed off in patches to reveal scales that had grown in below.

When the glow faded, he sat up and regarded his fellows. A long curved sword was placed in his hand. A voice spoke. "Welcome," it said.

Pauk hefted the blade. It felt natural and right. He gave his other arm a detached glance and was not surprised to see a writhing serpent where his hand had been. He opened his mouth and hissed, relishing the taste of the venom that dripped from the new fangs in his mouth. A new desire filled him. He wanted nothing more than to inflict pain and death, to sink his fangs into the flesh of another and watch them change.

Oh, but it felt good to be so strong.

Without another sound, he joined the other figures as they moved back into the deep swamp.

# PART 5

*"Within darkness they were placed and sealed away; these things of magic, so that none would know their dark temptations."*
—Qelekua Magebane, *The Cyrean Songs* 798 SA

From a tall hill more than a league from the city, Geril and Thrag watched the goings-on in Tulgesh. For most of the day they had remained just out of sight in a copse of ironwoods, observing the morehl army as it prepared to march to Balgavarr. The size of the horde was staggering, much larger than when the lava elves had captured the city, so reinforcements must have arrived from the distant homeland. This was a blow to Geril's confidence in the defenses of his home. An army of this magnitude would overwhelm the dwarf city in no time. He prayed the feral and frostwings would make it in time.

Looking up at Thrag, he noticed that his monstrous friend was watching the morehl through narrowed eyes and growling deep in his throat.

Long fangs were visible as the aereosa snarled. Geril almost smiled. The morehl had made a critical mistake when they fired their pistols on the king of the frostwings.

He turned back to the level plain below them. What had once been the green and fertile farmland of the selumari had been reduced to a trampled, muddy waste. While there were several tents and many fires, it was apparent that this was not to be a lasting camp. The lava elves were preparing to march and spending the last night with a minimum of tents so that they could leave all the quicker come morning. Most would sleep out in the open, by the fires. The morehl were spread out like a red and black blanket across the land. To Geril, the massed army looked like an infection that the land was powerless to excise.

The sooner they were driven back to the Uruzak Mountains, the better.

Thrag grunted behind him. "What is it?" he asked, turning. Thrag pointed to the skies over Tulgesh. Geril frowned, then realized what Thrag had noticed. The wyvern patrols that had flown over the city in regular patterns were gone. The last rider was circling his mount down into the city, leaving the sky empty but for a few scattered clouds. "Well and good," the dwarf said. "Let's hope they stay down after nightfall. Then we can fly in without being seen. Come, Thrag, let's get out of sight until dark." Thrag nodded and the two withdrew into the trees.

Once among the thick trucks, Geril sat down and contemplated what lay ahead. They had to get into the city unseen, search it for the hidden artifacts of the Magestorm, seal them away forever, and still escape without being captured or killed. He must have been out of his mind to agree to this.

Thrag was sprawled out, wings folded against his sides and casually scratching himself. Suddenly the beast was on his feet and staring intently into the trees. Geril was up in an instant, his warrior senses alerting him that they were not alone on this hill. He hefted his axe and waited, his stare fixed in the direction Thrag faced.

Slowly a tall figure emerged from the trees, moving cautiously. A long sword was held in both hands as the selumari trooper stepped into sight.

Geril relaxed, but only slightly. When the trooper saw the dwarf, she lowered her weapon a little and smiled apprehensively, her eyes never leaving Thrag.

"Greetings to you, vagha. I am Juna."

Geril lowered his axe. "Greetings, Juna. I am Geril sa'Ghuren, from Balgavarr. This is Thrag."

The coral elf nodded. "Your name is known. Matrek sent you to return with help. Where are the others?"

Geril shouldered his axe and shrugged. This was not going to go well.

"I am alone except for Thrag here."

Now the trooper frowned. "Alone? Matrek said that you would return with more warriors to help us retake Tulgesh. You return only with this… creature?" Thrag growled softly. It was possible that Thrag was seeing Juna as an enemy, despite the fact that Geril was not. Coral and lava elves bore some resemblance except for the color of their skin and hair. Thrag would be unaware of this and see only another type of elf that looked like the ones that had attacked him. "Easy, Thrag," Geril said, patting the thick hide. "Juna is a friend." He turned back to the elf. "Balgavarr has been found. None would come even if they could."

Juna had gasped hearing that the dwarf city had been discovered, and now nodded in understanding. "Those are unfortunate tidings. I'm afraid that Matrek will not be as sympathetic as I, though. He has awaited your return eagerly. He will not be pleased."

"I'm not concerned about Matrek," Geril said, forcing down his anger and scorn. "I have Balgavarr to think about."

"Then why are you and this… thing, here? Shouldn't you be in Balgavarr?" The tension was growing. It was thick in the air, and if the unease between the two warriors was not broken, it could lead to disastrous results. Geril sighed. "His name is Thrag, and I have my reasons," he said, "but I can only speak of them to Matrek. It may be important for both our races that he hears me. Is he near?"

Juna's shoulders slumped as the battle-readiness left her. "He is near," she said. "Less than a league from here we have a small camp in some hidden tunnels that the vagha among us dug. The rest of the army is scattered throughout the region, but Matrek wanted to stay close to the city. I was scouting and saw you fly in. I will take you to him." Without another word, she turned and walked into the trees. Thrag and Geril followed.

"Get out of my sight!" Matrek shouted. "I care not for your reasons, dwarf. Reasons will not give us back our home!" The selumari leader slumped onto his stool.

Geril waited until the fury faded from Matrek's eyes before speaking.

"You asked me to take word back to Balgavarr. Nothing was ever said about my returning with more warriors. I have done as you asked. My obligation to you is ended."

"Then why are you here?" The selumari champion was shouting and began a loud tirade about the undependability of all things vaghan.

Geril could understand the frustration Matrek was feeling. For weeks the selumari had cowered in hiding, far from their home. These tunnels were warm and dry, fine for a dwarf, but cramped and confining to a race that lived for the open air and broad seas. Many of the survivors had taken to calling the refuge Little Tulgesh, but never where Matrek might overhear. Behind the angry words, Geril could sense the frustration of the coral elf champion. The selumari were a proud race and to live in such rugged conditions must appall them. Even the chair he sat on had been hastily crafted from branches, as was the table. Crude, but efficient.

Matrek was pacing, his arms swinging angrily at his sides, his right hand occasionally grasping the hilt of his cutlass. His lips moved as he swore and muttered under his breath. Geril had not come here to be verbally beaten, and he was sorely tempted to get up and leave. However, much as he hated the fact, he still needed Matrek's help. "How many are left?" he asked.

Matrek whirled toward him so suddenly Geril flinched, expecting the grasping hand to draw the sword. "Why?" Matrek snarled.

"The morehl army is preparing to leave Tulgesh," Geril said. "I imagine they will leave only a token force behind. A surprise attack may catch what few remain unaware. Even a small battalion should be able to get into the city and seize control."

The fury faded from Matrek's face. His eyes darted from side to side as he considered Geril's words. "We are but few. The morehl hunt us for sport. Many of our finest warriors have been killed by roving patrols. Some of them shot from the air by riders. Still…" He leaned over and grasped the edge of the small table in the room. "There are maybe two score troopers and their hero commanders left alive. Almost all of the magic-users are dead, there are but three evokers left. Most of your people have left. A few footmen pledged to see this through and helped us dig these holes we hide in. All the mammoths were killed, but half a dozen lizard riders survived the last battle and hide in the woods. Your wizard Latkis was captured and is being held in the city."

Geril blinked. Latkis was a friend. "Why is the army moving out so soon after taking the city?" Matrek wondered aloud. "They know that we are in the area. Laman would not be so foolish as to leave now. What could draw him away?"

"Balgavarr has been found."

The words were ominous in the cramped room. Even Matrek was stunned. Balgavarr would indeed make a tempting prize for the morehl, who desired all precious metals and gems. Balgavarr had been dug inside a mountain thick with riches. It was also the best-defended city in this part of Esfah. If the morehl got a foothold there, they would never be driven from the land. "I see," Matrek said softly. "Forgive me, this is dire news."

"So you see why they make ready to march? Conqueror Laman must feel that you survivors are no threat, else he would not so readily abandon Tulgesh."

Matrek nodded. The dwarf made sense, but he could feel that Geril was holding something back. "You came all this way to tell me this? We would have seen sooner or later. What are you not telling me?"

Geril sighed. "The lava elves seek the relics of the Magestorm." There were several gasps from those selumari standing in the outer halls. Geril then related all that had happened to him since his departure from Tulgesh. When he heard of the frostwings and the new army of feral, Geril saw hope bloom in the champion's eyes. "Caulte told me to come," Geril finished. "He had a vision that the relics would be found. If they are, this part of our world will fall under the shadow of Death forever."

Geril waited for Matrek to spew his disbelief in the shaman's words. The champion instead surprised him by jerking upright and pointing to trooper nearby. "Find those evokers. Bring them here immediately."

Geril had never actually seen one of the selumari magicians up close before. During battle they usually stayed in the rear echelons and out of harm's way while they worked the elemental forces of Esfah. Unlike the vaghan wizards who knew the spells of earth and fire, the coral elf magic-users cast magic from the water and air that they themselves were made of. It was an altogether different magic than the vagha used, but just as powerful.

He had pictured them as warrior mages, clad in the silvery armor favored by the elves, and holding their staffs and wands high as they brought down lightning on the heads of their enemies, or walls of ice to protect their own troops.

The three evokers huddled close together under the scrutiny of the selumari champion. They were not as Geril had imagined them. These casters were clad only in thin green robes instead of the dark blue robes and silver armor of their superiors. Their spiked green hair was cropped short and they lacked the distinctive headdress of rank worn by the upper magic classes. They each wore a cutlass, but it was evident that they lacked familiarity with the weapons.

He knew enough to tell that these were the lowest caste of selumari magicians and considered little more than students. While capable of casting battle spells, it was harder for them to draw from the elemental forces of air and water than it was for their instructors. Their magic was not as reliable, but they were effective in large groups where they could combine their power. These three would not be much help in battle.

It was obvious that Matrek viewed them with little tolerance. As a warrior, magic was a powerful but unfamiliar tool to him. It lacked the solid feel of a good sword in the hand, but wielded by a schooled enchanter it was a deadly ally. A conjurer or enchanter was strong enough with the elements to be respected. Evokers were usually beneath his notice.

"I'm going to ask one question," Matrek said at last. "If you do not give me the answer I want, I'll have your worthless carcasses thrown from the camp."

The three elves withered under the hard glare of the champion. "Ask us, great Lord, and we will answer true," one of them replied.

Matrek sat down in the chair and leaned on the table. Running his hand through his long green hair, his eyes narrowed as he spoke. "What do you know of the Magestorm artifacts?"

As one, they stepped back. Their eyes were wide as they hurriedly whispered among themselves. The eldest among them stepped forward. "I am Saol. We will speak, Lord Matrek. What we can tell you is forbidden to those not of the arts, but we are all that remain. If what we know may be of service, our knowledge is yours."

Matrek smirked. "A wise choice. Where are they hidden?"

"This we do not know, Lord Matrek." Saol jumped back as Matrek grasped the hilt of his sword and snarled. He raised his hands in desperate supplication. "Please, my lord," he begged. "The exact knowledge was not given to us. We know only an ancient riddle."

Matrek released his sword. "Our home lies in ruin and the morehl walk the streets. The artifacts could very well help us retake our city. Speak this riddle. Perhaps we can puzzle it out together."

Geril looked at Matrek with alarm. The artifacts were supposed to be sealed away forever, not used in battle. What was the champion planning?

"I must warn you, Lord Matrek, that you will not remember what you hear. There is a spell within the riddle that prevents those without the gift from recalling it."

Matrek waved away the evoker's warning. "Let us see for ourselves."

Saol conferred with the other evokers for a moment, then stood tall and spoke. The moment he began, Geril felt an unusual gathering of energy in the small room, but none of the others said anything, so he kept quiet as well.

> *"When hearts attuned to wind and sea,*
> *To Esfah's youngest bend their knee*
> *Go where the arms of fire and earth*

*Once lent their aid to prove their worth.*

*The stone shall speak of many things,*
*But follow only myriad wings*
*To where the second's sign resides,*
*'Tis where the ancient power hides.*

*A maze made with an earthy skill*
*Waits for the sun to work its will,*
*For what has been in darkness sealed*
*Shall by light soon be revealed.*

*Then play the mage – a wave of fear,*
*A power quickly summoned here.*
*If open maw you wish to see,*
*The word unspoken is the key.*

*But take heed, you who wish this power—*
*You may bring Esfah's final hour."*

Matrek blinked. Several moments passed. "It seems you spoke truly, Saol. I can't remember a single word. Is there any other clue to the relics?"

Saol shrugged. "We do not know, milord. Perhaps the enchanters may have known, but they never spoke of one. They said that the student who could decipher the riddle would rise above the rest."

Geril's mind was whirling. He could remember the riddle, and the words made some sense to him. He could not understand Matrek's confusion.

Yet when the champion turned his gaze on the young dwarf, he merely shrugged. Matrek scowled and looked away, perplexed.

"This is of little help to us," the champion sighed. "We have wasted our time. Return to whatever books you salvaged from Tulgesh. Perhaps you may discover more clues to the answer." He looked to Geril again, and for the first time, his eyes were not hard. "Go home," he said. "You will be needed at Balgavarr Reaches. I apologize for my hasty words, friend dwarf. I would not be the cause of animosity between our people. You have kept your word; I can ask no more."

Geril bowed his head. "Thank you, but I cannot return home until I have done what I came to do. I must find the Magestorm relics and seal them away forever."

The champion blinked. "Friend Geril," he said, "the relics could turn the tide of this war. We could drive the morehl and the trogs from our lands forever."

"If they fall into the hands of our enemies, they could destroy us utterly," Geril countered.

"That is a risk I'm willing to take," Matrek said, his voice becoming sharp. "You can help us, or leave. If you stay, I may share some of the relics with you, even though they belong to my race."

Geril was on his feet before he could stop himself. "Your race?" he shouted. "I am no student, Matrek, but I know the legend of the Magestorm. All of the elder races commissioned the weapons that the gnomes made. My people did, your people did, even the damned morehl and trogs had weapons of magic and metal built by the gremmlobahnd who were often forced into service. We were all to blame! After the war ended it was decided to hide them in a place where they could never easily be found. My people helped build the place where..." his voice trailed off and he looked down at his feet. At the earth beneath his feet. "My people," he whispered.

Matrek watched him closely. Initially he had been taken aback at the dwarf's outburst and was fighting his own shame at the selfish way he was acting over who had the right to possess and control the relics. He heard the wisdom in the words of the vaghan soldier, but his own need to deal out a mighty vengeance on the red invaders was a powerful urge that was hard to resist. He was certain that he could use the relics wisely, and that none of them would find their way into the hands of the morehl. His people would do as he directed them to. Nothing, not even an honor-bound dwarf, would stop him. Now Geril was staring at his feet and whispering to himself.

Geril suddenly looked up, and his eyes bored into those of the selumari champion. What Matrek saw there caused him to step back, for the force evident in that gaze was staggering. In those eyes he saw what he knew to be understanding. The dwarf had figured out a part of the riddle! He grasped the hilt of his sword and yanked it free. "You remember the words, don't you? Tell me what you know," he said.

Geril's axe was in his hands faster than thought. "I don't know anything," he lied. "I have a suspicion, but it's not worth talking about. It won't help you, and neither will I. The relics must not be used, Matrek. I will do what I must in order to make sure that doesn't happen."

Matrek smirked. "Seize him," he said quietly. "Do not hurt him, but he doesn't leave until he tells what he knows."

Two troopers moved to grab the vaghan, but Geril was a trained warrior of his race. He drove the end of the axe handle into the gut of the nearest elf, driving the soldier back into the rough wall gasping for breath. He whirled and grabbed the thin armor of the second trooper. Thick dwarven muscles bulged as he lifted the elf off his feet and flung him across the small room to crash into Matrek. Both the table and chair shattered into splinters as the elves tumbled to the floor. Geril surveyed the ruin with a grim smile, then bolted down the tunnel to the outside. The rest of the elves watching were too stunned to move.

Behind him came loud shouts and angry cries. He bolted, running as fast as he could. Matrek was not known to be forgiving. He burst through the thick bushes that hid the entrance and into the open, startling Thrag.

Thrag had been napping in the bright sunshine and Geril's abrupt exit caused him to leap to his feet with a near-roar, scattering twigs and thin branches that had been placed across him like a blanket. The black wings spread wide and long spears of ice formed in each hand. Then the beast saw that it was his small friend. The ice spears were casually dropped to the ground, already melting in the warm sun.

Juna had been guarding the entrance and keeping an eye on Thrag as Matrek had ordered her to do. When the creature stretched out and went to sleep, she relaxed. However, the big brute was plainly visible, and she was afraid a random flying patrol might spot him and thus discover the hidden tunnel. So she fought boredom by scouting the area for branches and twigs and used them to cover up the bulk of the beast.

Thrag had opened an eye when he felt the first branches touch him, but he perceived no threat from the blue elf, and went back to napping.

Now he swept Geril into a protective embrace and bared his fangs at the hidden entrance. Juna ran up and was surprised to find the blade of a wickedly sharp battle-axe held at her throat. The dwarf's eyes bored into hers, and her heart quailed. In those gold eyes she saw the face of Death. "I count you a friend, Juna," the vaghan whispered, "don't make me kill you."

She slowly backed away. "Go," she said. "I won't try to stop you."

Geril's eyes softened. "Good. When you think of me, remember that I tried to do the right thing." She nodded, but held up her hand.

"I know what it is you intend to do," she said.

A frown crossed the rough features of the dwarf. "Is that so?"

She smiled and pointed at her large pointed ears. "The selumari have sharp hearing. My father used to tell me tales of the Magestorm. It gave me horrible nightmares. Matrek must not gain the power of the relics." She chuckled at his surprised expression. Then turned as a chorus of yells came from the hidden tunnel. "Time grows short. Do you desire my help? Not all the coral elves crave battle and domination the way Matrek does."

Geril turned to Thrag. "She comes with us," he said. "Can you carry us both?"

Thrag responded by lifting Geril to his shoulders. Once the dwarf was firmly seated, Thrag gently grasped Juna around the middle and lifted her off her feet. Juna felt as helpless as a babe in the grip of the beast. She could feel the strength and power in his hands, yet she was held so carefully she did not fear injury.

Thrag took several loping hops as his wings beat the air. Juna let out a muffled squeal as he left the earth with a grunt and struggled into the sky as selumari warriors broke from the tunnel. With several mighty flaps, Thrag flew back and over the tunnel, his wide black wings scything through the air and lifting them out of sight. The soldiers failed to see them winging away.

To the troopers, their quarry had simply vanished.

Matrek stepped from the tunnel and looked around. He saw nothing but the emptiness of the hills, and a few trees scattered here and there. Where could the dwarf have gone? His anger seethed and boiled beneath the calm veneer he showed the troops. He held the fury in, relishing the feeling of power that the wrath infused him with. That a vaghan could so easily take him and several soldiers by surprise was unsettling.

He grabbed the nearest trooper and spun the elf around. "The beast that accompanied the dwarf, the frostwing, where is it?"

The trooper shrugged. "I do not know, Lord Champion. Perhaps it carried the vaghan away."

Matrek stared at the sky, slowly turning to look in every direction. If they were airborne, they were long gone from normal sight. "Perhaps," he mused. "How many eagle knights remain?"

The trooper thought a moment. "Four, milord. They hide in the forest of Cheroon. Shall I send a horseman and summon them here?"

"Yes. It seems they will be going hunting."

Thrag came to earth far from the refuge, and near Tulgesh. The landing was not the usual gentle touchdown he'd come to expect from Thrag. Instead, it was a bone jarring, barely controlled crash. The areosa let go of Juna just before impact, and the trooper hit the ground rolling, springing lightly to her feet. Geril's teeth slammed together painfully and his upper body jerked forward. If not for his knees being so firmly locked around Thrag's neck, he would have tumbled off. *Maybe that would have been better,* he thought.

He climbed down and took a deep breath, relieved to have survived another flight. Thrag was walking slowly around on all fours, lifting each leg, and shaking the foot before setting it gingerly back down. As a youth, Geril had several times tried to jump from too great a height and knew how badly Thrag's feet were tingling. He stifled laughter and turned away before it could escape. Juna was rubbing her sides and muttering.

He sent a quick prayer of thanks to Eldurim that they had not been seen. Flying so close to the city was risky even with the wyvern patrols apparently being recalled and the sentries along the walls around the city missing. Dusk was rapidly approaching, and yet the morehl were acting much more carelessly than he expected. They were growing much too confident.

Juna brushed herself off and straightened her armor. Despite how carefully she had been carried her sides hurt, and she rubbed them gently.

"Now what?" she asked.

Geril stretched the kinks out of his legs and grinned. "I wish I knew."

"Perfect," Juna grumped as she sat down. "Matrek will never pardon me for betraying him, and you don't know what to do next."

Geril chuckled. Reaching up, he patted her shoulder. "Tell him I forced you to come along. He might believe that." He looked up toward the city. "I guess our first move is to try to figure out the riddle. That may give us a starting place."

"What riddle?"

"I thought you said you had sharp hearing."

She rolled her eyes. "I didn't stand there with my ear to the tunnel for the entire time."

He repeated the riddle, but the words vanished from her mind almost as quickly as Geril spoke them. He noted her confused expression with a wry grin before explaining. "Latkis told me I had an aptitude for magic, and one day I would have to choose which path to follow and become either a wizard or a warlord. That may be why I can remember it. As for the riddle, the first part I understand. *Hearts attuned to wind and sea* refers to your race, the selumari. *Esfah's youngest* has to be the morehl, as they are the youngest of the Elder races. *Arms of fire and earth* can only be my people, the vagha."

"What is the next part?" Juna asked.

*"Once lent their aid to prove their worth,"* Geril responded. "That has to be a reference to the Magestorm war, and how our two races fought the armies of Death together."

Juna smacked her fist against her knee as she sat down on a rock. "Of course," she said, "when the alliance was first formed between Tulgesh and Balgavarr. The final battle of the Magestorm war was fought in the fields outside the city. This isn't so hard," she grinned.

Geril leaned back against an ironwood tree and slowly slid to the ground. "By Eldurim's beard, I'm tired," he said wearily. He watched with amusement as Thrag folded his wings and flopped to the ground with a dust- raising thud. Resting his head on one thick forearm, the areosa was soon snoring heavily.

Geril chuckled and shook his head, wishing he could sleep so easily at any time. He ran his fingers through the length of his beard and considered the next phrase in the riddle. *"The stone shall speak of many things,"* he spoke aloud. "I wonder what that means."

Juna sat down next to him; the broad flat leaves of the ironwood casting a comfortable shade from the blazing, late afternoon sun. Crossing her long, slender legs, she plucked a blade of sweet sugargrass and stuck it between her teeth thoughtfully, all the while watching the leaves above her. Ironwoods were notorious for dropping their heavy foliage on unwary folk. The leaves fell hard and fast and caused painful bruises. "It's funny how I can't remember a single line until you tell me the next one. Interesting magic."

Removing her helmet, she ran her hands through her spiky green hair. She lay back and crossed her arms under her head.

"Do the selumari have a talking stone? Perhaps an oracular statue?"

She frowned. "Not that I know of, but I never did care to meddle in the affairs of magic users. Your people know more of stone than mine."

Geril considered a moment. "Stones do not speak in Balgavarr. This grows more frustrating with every breath," he growled. "How can a stone have a mouth?"

Juna sat up. "Of course!" she nearly shouted, jumping to her feet.

Geril opened one eye and regarded her with amusement. "You have a thought?"

She reached down and grabbed his arm, dragging him to his feet. She pointed to the city. "In the temple," she said excitedly. "In the temple of Ailuril there is a doorway that looks like a mouth!"

Geril was stunned. Could it be so easy? "Does it speak?" he asked.

Juna looked at him with disgust. "It only looks like a mouth, you vaghan imbecile. Beyond and below are the catacombs. Where better to hide the relics?"

Geril smiled. "Where indeed? Now how do we get in?"

"When night falls, we should be able to slip in unseen. Thrag's fur is very dark, I doubt anyone will see us."

"True, but they will hear us. Thrag can carry me in without noise, but with both of us I doubt we can land without alerting the entire city."

Juna whirled around to face her small companion. "I will not be left behind, Geril. We don't need to fly to get into the city. Besides, do you know where the temple is?" She lifted her chin and stared down her nose at him.

He shrugged. "I have to admit that I don't. Alright, we'll need a plan. It's your home, what do you suggest?"

She hunched down and using her finger drew a crude drawing of Tulgesh in the dirt. "Listen," she said.

# PART 6

*"Make no bargains with the beings of shadow, for they know not honor."*
*—Semis the Wizened, selumari priest of Ailuril*

The morehl were restless in their camp outside the city. Very few sought their bedrolls as the excitement of the coming battle and victory kept their black hearts pumping with bloodlust. Most of them spent the time sharpening the edge of their blades, or making extra lead balls for their pistols. Many more gathered around enormous bonfires and bragged of how many dwarves they would kill, how many more they had killed in past wars, and the riches they would carry from the vaghan city.

Laman moved through the scattered groups of his soldiers, pleased at what he heard. He kept the hood of his cloak pulled close around his face and stepped softly. Many times in past wars he had uncovered plots against himself by doing this. Each time the conspirators had died wondering how he had discovered their schemes. None would have believed so simple an answer.

The sentries at the gates let him pass unchallenged, familiar with his nightly excursions. The majority of the troops were camped outside the city, while the officers took temporary residence in the richer of the selumari houses. He had made himself comfortable in the governor's large home near the center of the city.

Most of the city lay in ruin. He walked past smoking timbers and stepped around broken stone. The troops took great pleasure in putting to fire anything they were covetous of. The hatred all of them felt for the prosperity of the coral elves fueled the need for wanton destruction. He saw it only as a waste, but the devastation also served another purpose.

Once through the gates he walked a direct line to the palatial estate.

Back home this house would have been considered a dwelling for the members of the royal family. That it had once belonged to a mere city official astounded him. He scarcely glanced at the head mounted on a pike in the front garden. Tiny eatum bugs flew in clouds around it, undisturbed by his passing. The bulging eyes and gaping mouth of the former governor were no longer worth any of his attention. He had decided not to have it removed, although the smell was becoming intense.

He took the steps to the main door two at a time, but stopped abruptly upon reaching the top. Both guards lay either unconscious or dead just inside the door, their weapons sheathed. Nothing moved beyond the bladesmen, and the interior was no longer brightly lit. How had he failed to notice that from the road?

The vorpal sword hummed as he drew it from the scabbard. It was almost as if the weapon could sense a nearby enemy. He moved silently through the open door, his steps cautious and wary. A quick search of the first level yielded no intruders. He wanted to relax his guard, but to do so prematurely would be foolhardy. There were still two more floors. For the first time he cursed his own arrogance at choosing such a large house for himself. What did he need with so many rooms? He was a soldier, not a politician.

The stairs to the next floor were clear as he started up. Halfway to the top, the raw odor of decay filled his nostrils and he winced. His heart was beating furiously as he reached the last step and turned the corner to the room he had made into his provisional office. The anticipation of thwarting an assassin and making an example of them caused him to smile grimly. He leapt into the room, sword held ready.

The lich regarded him coldly with blank, dead eyes. "I take it my visit is unexpected?" The undead mage stood behind the desk, arms crossed and hidden within the folds of its robes. Despite the mummified appearance, the conqueror recognized that this creature had once been a selumari enchanter.

The skin that had once been blue with life was now a mottled gray. Patches of mold grew in the hollow of the throat. Beneath the hooded cloak it wore, the empty eye sockets glowed with red malice and a hatred for all things living.

He suppressed a shudder and lowered the sword. "Your boldness is surprising, not your presence. How did you get past the sentries at the gates?"

"We can move unseen when we wish." The voice was as harsh as rubbing rocks together. "Your house guards proved more observant, but they will recover." A bony arm lifted and gestured to the shadows in the far corner of the room.

The death knight stepped from the darkness. The reek of rotting flesh was overpowering. The knight was taller and broader in the shoulders than either coral or lava elves, and by the heavy plate armor it wore Laman assumed that it had once been an amazon war chief. Faint wisps of hair clung to the bone of the skull, along with dried pieces of skin. He kept the sword down, but only because the knight's weapon remained in the scabbard. "Why are you here?" he demanded.

"I have come to see that our agreement continues to be honored. What progress have you made?"

"None. Other matters occupy my time. Balgavarr Reaches has been found. The army marches at sunrise."

The withered flesh stretched into a frown. "You promised us the death relics once Tulgesh was taken. We aided your conquest of Seshara because it brought you closer to a victory here. Now you dare break the covenant?"

The conqueror grew uncomfortable. The knight was blocking the only escape from the room, and though the sword remained sheathed, it did not negate the possible danger. Some of the undead could move quickly when they needed to. "The Magestorm artifacts are hidden well. I have had soldiers searching since we took the city. Have you not seen them tearing down almost every structure?"

"Time grows short, Laman. If you wish our assistance at Balgavarr, find the relics."

"That was not the agreement. You are to help us take this part of Esfah entirely, then we give you the death relics." He approached the Lich slowly, his sword pointed to the floor. The death knight's head followed him, its neck bones creaking. "Why don't you know where they are? You were once one of them."

The lich unfolded its arms and leaned on the desk. The glow from its eyes seemed to grow brighter. "What I once was is unimportant. Nothing from my previous existence remains. That is what it means to be one of the undead. Would you like to see for yourself?"

Laman smiled. "Do not attempt to frighten me with empty threats. You need me as much as I need you. You may have gotten into the city unobserved, but you may find it more difficult to leave. The artifacts will be found soon, I can assure you of that. But if your legion does not fight with us at Balgavarr, the undead will get nothing. I will see to that."

The lich nodded slowly. "There is another matter."

Laman stepped back and slid the vorpal sword back into the scabbard. He moved to the window and opened the shutters to get more air into the room.

"What would that be?"

"You form dangerous alliances."

Laman blinked. How did this thing know? "I don't know what you mean," he said, but heard the untruth in his own voice.

"You may find the scalders less than dependable."

It knew, so there was no more point in deceit. "What do you know of the scalders?"

The lich lowered itself into the chair behind the desk. "They are a new race of Esfah. We have encountered them before. Truly, they are fierce opponents that crave combat. They are loyal to none. If the battle shifts, you may find them aiding your enemies at the first opportunity. They are not children of Lord Death, as you and I. He sought their power but found it incorruptible. They care only for their own needs. Whatever reasons they have for joining with you, be certain there is another they will not speak of."

"That is not your concern. Getting the legion to Balgavarr is. How many troops will be there?"

"Enough. More awaken each day to Death's call. You might even… recognize some of them." The lich stared at him, waiting for a reaction.

Laman wouldn't give it the satisfaction. "That doesn't bother me. The uncertainty of whether or not I can trust you does."

Rising from the chair, the lich moved silently across the room to the open door. "We will meet in the foothills below Balgavarr. The legion will be ready, but I warn you. If the scalders turn on us, I will hold you responsible."

Laman nodded. "So be it," he said. Then a sudden realization struck him. "I haven't told you where Balgavarr is. Would you like a map?"

A rasping chuckle filled the room. "As you have already surmised, we already know where the vaghan city lies. We always have. Find the relics and find them soon. The next time we meet I will not be so tolerant of your failure." It turned surprisingly fast and swept through the door, making no noise as it descended the steps. The death knight followed close behind, but not as quietly.

Laman breathed his relief. Only in the presence of the undead did he feel a hint of fear. They were an enigma of Esfah, and one of the strongest of the races. It was unlikely that any dwarves would survive the coming battle with the legion fighting alongside his troops and the trogs. Such a victory would be sweet.

As for giving his rotting allies any Magestorm relics, well… he would deal with that when the time came. Some items would have to be surrendered to be sure, but if the undead thought they were going to get all the death relics, then they were sorely mistaken. Once he had possession of the Magestorm weapons, the morehl would control this part of Esfah forever.

Riches and glory would be his.

The air in the room was at last clearing. He sat at the desk and stared at the maps spread out on the surface. Tulgesh was plainly marked on the coast and north of that in the Kafnysan Mountains he had written in the word Balgavarr. He stared at the word for some time before rolling up the map. He was certain that a few days hence he would be emptying the coffers of the dwarf city.

So why did he suddenly have such a feeling of uncertainty?

Juna, Geril and Thrag crept along the city wall. It was still some time before the moon rose, so they were well hidden in the shadows. So far they had not encountered any sentries, but it was best not to become overconfident and reveal themselves to a wayward patrol they had failed to see.

The selumari trooper had waited until full dark to lead them through the trees to the wall. Geril had chafed at their slow advance, but he had decided to trust Juna and her plan to get them into Tulgesh. He wasn't as sure it would work, but he was unable to think of a better idea. The trip through the trees to this small unused gate had been nerve-wracking with Juna stopping at every noise, real or imagined. The dwarf was astonished that the morehl had no guards patrolling the area around the coral elf city. Could they really be so foolish as to think that all resistance had been eliminated?

Juna halted suddenly and reached back to Geril, her hand gentle but firm on the shoulder of her shorter companion. "Sentries," she whispered.

Geril nodded. It was about time. He lifted his axe from where it rested against his shoulders. "How many?"

She held up two fingers. "I see the footprints of only one squad. There is no way to tell how long before they will be relieved, if at all. It's a chance we have to take. They have to be removed." Her voice was the softest murmur.

Geril grinned in the darkness as a breeze brushed his neck. "I don't have any problems killing lava elves. How close can we get before they see us?"

"Very close. Can you keep your big friend quiet?"

Geril turned to whisper instructions to Thrag. "Damn," he said, almost too loudly.

Juna hissed a warning. "What is it?"

"Thrag is gone. I didn't hear him leave." He shrugged unhappily. What could he have done?

Juna lowered her head. "I hope he knows what he's doing," she said. "If they sound any alarm, all will be lost."

A dark shape hurtled by overhead. Geril looked up and chuckled softly.

"Somehow I don't think that's going to be a problem."

The sentries were caught completely by surprise. Bored by a night of pacing, they were unaware that Death was coming for them. Thrag flew to a height far above them and dove, his wings tucked close to his body for more speed.

Just above the earth he straightened into a rapid, level glide, coming up behind them. Stretching his arms forward, he caught each elf by the throat and lifted them off their feet. Their air cut off, neither made a sound as they were borne skyward, their swords dropped and forgotten. Thrag's wings cut the air forcefully and he grunted with each stroke as he lifted the weight.

Far below, Geril heard a wet tearing noise, then the soft pattering of drops on the earth. He knew better than to think it was raindrops. Two thick thuds reached his ears and he winced. The sentries had met a swift and terrible end.

Thrag landed quietly behind him. His claws and fangs were stained with thick black blood. Geril reached up and patted the broad shoulder. "Well done, my friend," he said. "Next time warn us first, alright?"

"The way is clear," Juna said, getting back to the business at hand. "You will need to help me now, and we'll need more light." From inside her cloak she removed two small clay jars. Removing the corks, she inspected the contents and nodded.

"Are you sure this will work?" Geril asked as he pulled the sightstone from its pouch. Holding the magic gem in his closed palm, he concentrated.

"It has before. Several of us have gotten into the city this way to scavenge for food and weapons. In the dark I doubt anyone will look too closely." She noticed he wasn't replying and looked up. The dwarf was deep in meditation and swaying slightly. Understanding that he was working magic, she waited with as much patience as she could.

After a moment, Geril opened his eyes. Hanging in the air before him floated his starry motes: how magic presented itself to the dwarf's mind when he tried to summon it. He nearly cursed.

There was hardly any there, and it was only red. None of it was useful for earth magic.

This far from the highlands, he was unable to summon much of the magic force of Esfah through the stone. It was enough for his purpose, though it was still disconcerting to know that so little magic was available to him, even with the stone in his possession. Geril felt Juna watching him and knew she was unable to see his motes. "It's working," he said, and relief spread across her face. "I can give us a little light, but it probably won't last long."

"A moment is all I need," she said. "Hurry."

Geril reached up and cupped the mote in his empty hand while the other grasped the sightstone tightly. "*Avok a lumen*," he whispered. Light shot from between his closed fingers and Juna gasped. Opening his hand, he let a little more light spill from his palm. He panted with the effort of the spell.

"Be quick," he warned. "I am not even an apprentice theurgist, so I can't keep this glowing long."

Juna nodded and removed her helm before unfastening her cloak, then unlaced her shirt. Geril quickly looked away before he saw more of her than she wished seen. Dipping her fingers into the larger of the two jars, she scooped out the red paste it held. She smeared it over her hands and arms, then her face, neck and chest. The soft blue of her skin changed to the ruddy red hue of the morehl. Geril put the sightstone away. He poured the contents of the smaller jar over her head. He used his fingers to work the oily liquid across her scalp, watching with amusement as her hair turned from green to black. He sat back and grinned. "How do I look?" she asked.

"Very ugly," he said. He exhaled a loud breath as the light spell winked out.

In truth she was still quite lovely, even in the disguise of their enemy. Thrag growled behind him and looking back he saw the furry face watching Juna with confusion. "It's okay, Thrag," he said. "It is still our friend." The devastator shook his head and wandered into the darkness.

Juna stripped off her armor. Beneath, she wore a simple tunic and trousers. Unbuckling her sword belt, she handed the weapon to Geril before putting on one of the morehl blades that had been dropped. "With luck, any guards we encounter will not notice my lack of armor."

There was a thump behind her as Thrag appeared out of the darkness.

Before him on the ground was the lava elf armor that one of the sentries had been wearing. He pointed to it and then to Juna. "Good idea, Thrag," she said. "This will help." She quickly put on the strange armor, wincing as the weight settled on her shoulders. Picking up the helm, she wiped away the black blood with her sleeve. Once placed on her head, she no longer looked like a coral elf. Only her non black eyes betrayed her race, and in the dark Geril doubted anyone would notice.

He walked over to Thrag and scratched the thick chest. Thrag purred. "Fly above us, my friend. Do not attack unless you see we are being pursued. Wait for me to wave to you before you land. Do you understand?" He smiled as Thrag nodded and took to the air.

Juna drew the poniard and hefted the weapon. "Good blade," she remarked. "Let's hope I don't have to use it."

Geril turned and handed Juna his axe. "I hope this works," he said, his face grim. "I don't want to find myself on the wrong end of an executioner's blade."

She shrugged. "If it doesn't, I'll be right there beside you."

Walking through the rubble-strewn streets of Tulgesh was a shock. Geril remembered when he had first seen the picturesque coastal city of the selumari. Fresh from the long march from Balgavarr, his spirit had been refreshed by the beauty before him.

The city surrounded a natural cove almost a full league across and was itself enclosed by a wall several spans high. The water of the cove was crystalline blue and as still as glass. Floating on the water and in the air above it were many of the wondrous coral ships the elves used to explore the seas and the rest of the world. It was in these ships that their ancestors had traveled from the Birthlands to this cove. Here they had built a majestic city marveled at by the other races. Even the homes of the lower classes were well kept and clean. Being used to the underground streets and stone houses of Balgavarr, Geril had stood in awe of the selumari city.

Now he could sense the horror and heartbreak Juna was feeling as she surveyed the ruin of her home. Even at this late hour, soldiers continued their destruction and looting by torchlight while they searched for loot and the magic items their leader sought.

So far they had only been stopped once, at the gates, and Juna's story of capturing a vaghan spy had been waved off with indifference. Apparently other patrols brought in prisoners regularly. They had pointed the way to the temporary prison and then dismissed Juna with bored salutes.

On the streets, the bodies of the dead lay where they had fallen. The dead of the morehl had been taken from the city. Some were given honorable burials; those considered worthy had been sent back to Uruzak to have their remains honored in their great halls: propped up in their galleries of heroes. The morehl's enemies were left to rot. The stench of death and decay was almost overpowering. Geril turned his eyes from the pathetic corpses and swallowed bile.

"Why do the gods allow them to do this to us?" she whispered.

Geril had no answer for her, so he chose to change the subject. "Are we near the temple?"

"Not far," she replied. "You can just see the towers."

The dwarf looked up, and in the bright light of the moon he could discern the twin towering spires of the temple looming over the rooftops. His sparse knowledge of selumari beliefs recalled the northern tower as being devoted to Ailuril, and the southern tower to Aguarehl. Each had its own set of priests and priestesses, and their own rites and practices. It had been from the top of these that the invading horde of the lava elves had first been sighted.

Now as they approached the impressive structure, Geril felt fear beginning to squeeze around his heart. This had been far too simple. How had they come so far without being challenged more often? Only a few had even bothered with them. The few soldiers they had seen had barely glanced at them before going back to whatever they were doing. He could hear the sharp hiss of breath Juna took whenever a morehl came near. She held a sword at his back, feigning herself ready to use it on Geril, and then removed it when they were ignored.

In moments the ruined iron gates of the temple loomed before them. Both halves lay twisted and broken just inside the courtyard. At the far end of the courtyard lay the shattered remains of the ironwood doors. The thick smell of wyverns stung their noses. A large bonfire burned in the center of the courtyard, and in its light they saw more than a dozen of the winged steeds curled up around the walls. The riders slept close to the fire. Juna gasped when she beheld the desecration of the selumari holy place. A single tear rolled down her face and she wiped it away angrily.

"How do we get past them?" Geril whispered.

She spoke through clenched teeth. "Quietly, unless you have some magic that can make us fly?"

Geril shook his head. "There's very little of the magic I know in these lands. I was fortunate to draw enough to give us that small light spell."

A shadow passed over them with a whisper and a swirling of dust. Geril looked up to see a dark form circling against the bright pinpoints of the stars.

He smiled grimly. Somehow, with Thrag near, his courage was bolstered. He looked at the high stone walls around the temple. They were unusual because the selumari rarely worked with wood, leaving stonework to the vagha whom… He smacked his fist into his hand. "Of course!" his voice was sharp, and Juna poked him with the sword. "Quiet," she warned. "Do you want to wake them all?"

The dwarf pointed to the wall. "That is vaghan made or I'm a selumari fisherman." He winced and looked over his shoulder. Juna appeared not to have noticed his use of the old insult. He was glad the darkness hid his blush of embarrassment. "Come on," he said, and started toward the outer part of the wall before Juna could think to follow him. With a whispered curse, she went after him.

Geril made his way around the wall until they were behind the temple. His eyes scanned up and down as he rubbed his hands over the surface. Juna could not imagine what the dwarf was looking for, especially with only the starlight to see by. In the dim light the wall looked smooth as an eggshell to her. Near the back of the temple, Geril uttered a small laugh. The elven trooper watched with amazement as his hand appeared to sink into the solid surface of the stone. There was a barely audible click, and then the muted sound of grinding gears. As she watched, a portion of the wall only Geril's height slid back, revealing a small dark opening. Musty unused air wafted out, making both of them wince. "By the gods," she whispered, "what is that? How did you put your hand into the wall?"

Geril grinned. "My people never build a wall without at least one back door. Your priests would have known about this, but those who dwell here were told to keep the knowledge to themselves." He pointed to the wall. The surface was unflawed, and Juna shook her head and admitted she couldn't see anything. Geril touched the wall again, and the tips of his fingers disappeared into the surface. Juna touched the wall where he did and gasped as her fingers vanished into the wall. "It's called a rockblanket," Geril explained. "The wizards make them. Tiny pebbles are strung on thin wire and hung over openings we wish to cover. We use them to hide switches like the one for this door. If you don't know what to look for, you'll never see one."

"Very clever," she said. "Now let's finish this."

"Agreed." Geril looked in. Narrow steps led down into thicker shadows. "It's a short walk, but it should take us directly into the temple. No one will see us. Better than tip-toeing through a full courtyard of trained morehl soldiers."

With a muffled thump, Thrag came to earth behind them. He scanned the area quickly before loping closer. Quizzically he looked at his small friend standing before the secret passage. "No," he growled, baring his teeth. His heavy hand grasped Geril's shoulder and pulled him back.

Geril shrugged him off. "There's no other way for us to get in, Thrag," he said. "It's safe, but you may be too big to follow."

Thrag nodded his understanding, but the disapproval on his furry face was clear. His wings folded tight against his body. "I go," he rasped.

Geril smiled at his friend. "Very well, but if you get stuck I'm not staying behind to pull you out." With that said he motioned for Juna to hand him his axe, and once secured to his back, he tried to step inside but was stopped by Thrag. Shaking his head, the winged warrior moved past the two of them, stooped over, and entered the tunnel; his broad shoulders brushed the sides of the entrance. Geril grinned at Juna and stepped in. Juna shook her head and followed.

Down the steps and inside the passageway, the thick stone that surrounded them shut out the familiar sounds of the night. The stygian darkness was thicker than the dank mud of Deepmire. Both of them walked blindly, their hands held out before them. The tunnel sloped downward at first, then leveled off for more paces than Geril could count. From the rich, earthy smell, he guessed they were now under the gardens behind the temple. Ahead he could hear Thrag moving slowly down the subterranean corridor. The devastator was grunting as he forced his way down the narrow passage, unaware of the dust he was raising. Both Geril and Juna covered their noses to keep from sneezing. When the devastator looked back, the two glowing red eyes startled Geril. At least Thrag could see where he was going.

The floor sloped up rapidly and abruptly ended when Geril walked into Thrag. There was not enough space to squeeze around. "Are there steps going up, Thrag?"

There was a low rumble in Thrag's throat as he spoke. "Yesss."

"Can you reach the top?" The tunnel was getting stuffy, and Geril was starting to feel claustrophobic, which was unusual for a dwarf.

"Yesss."

"Good. Look for a lever and pull it towards you." He felt Thrag move, then heard the squeak of a lever moving and the same working of gears. Dim light spilled into the tunnel as the exit ground open over countless years of accumulated dust. To those in the tunnel the sound was alarmingly loud, and both the dwarf and the elf expected an armed group of guards to descend on them in force. Each breathed a sigh of relief when nothing happened, and then both of them covered their noses and moaned as the thick smell of dung wafted into the tunnel.

Thrag pulled his bulk through the exit first and stood tall. Geril and Juna crept out with weapons in hand. Looking around, they saw that they had emerged behind the altar from the base of what had been a marble statue of Ailuril. The altar and a large area around it were covered with a tall pile of wyvern manure. Firelight from the courtyard and a few lanterns hanging on the walls cast enough light inside for them to see by. Dim to be sure, but just enough. Geril looked over the base and found the rockblanket that concealed the lever in the base. The hidden door slid shut when he pulled it, the sound of its movement hardly more than a whisper in the large temple. He looked up to find Juna staring in horror at what the morehl and trogs had done to the interior of the temple. Thoughts of comforting her fled his mind. Better to let her fury and hatred grow. He almost pitied the invader that crossed her path. At last she shook her head and shrugged, "This will be undone, I swear it." She pointed at the wall to their right and the opening in it. "There is the doorway. It is called the Ahymoc Eldurim."

Geril nodded. "The road of Eldurim." The aperture certainly looked like a mouth. Large stones outlined the opening, giving the appearance of teeth about to bite. Steep stairs descended into blackness beyond it. Set in the wall above were two carvings, shaped like eyes and filled with blue and green glass. In the center of each carved eye was what appeared to be a single large quartz crystal. Unlike the beautiful artwork the selumari were renowned for, this was almost hideous. He suppressed a shudder.

Juna removed a lantern from the wall near the doorway. Holding it up they both could see the runes carved into each stone tooth. Geril recognized both selumari and vaghan symbols carved deep into each rock face. He touched one fearfully, as if it would burn his fingers. The stone was cold and rough and completely harmless. He almost laughed out loud. Then his fingers brushed an emblem of a small winged creature he knew to be a symbol for magic. "What is this one?" he whispered.

Juna leaned in closer. "That is the sign of the sprites. Creatures of magic that sometimes fight with us. None of them have been seen for many years."

The dwarf's eyes narrowed. "Sprites? Would they be fairies?"

"Yes, I suppose they would."

"Wings," he said. "Follow only myriad wings. Hold the lantern inside the door."

Curiously, Juna did as he asked. The steps down were indeed very steep and set into each stone was the symbol of the sprites. "Follow them indeed," he said. "This is the way, I'm sure of it." His eyes roamed over the walls inside the doorway, pausing on a single stone on the opposite wall that reflected the lantern light. "Mirrorstone? Why would there be mirrorstone here?"

Juna looked over his shoulder. "What is mirrorstone?"

Geril pointed to the single rock set near the junction of roof and wall. "That is a mirrorstone, a kind of rock that reflects light. The stronger the light, the brighter it is reflected. Bright sunlight makes it too bright to look upon. We use it to light the deeper shafts of our mines by placing it at different levels and angling it to pass the light from one stone to the next."

He looked back over his shoulder at the far wall of the temple. His sharp eyesight picked out another mirrorstone, but larger than the first. "This grows stranger by the moment," he said. Backing up from the mouth, he cast his gaze again to the carved eyes above it. The stone on the far wall was only slightly lower than the eyes. "Of course," he whispered.

Juna shook her head at his mutterings. "We're wasting time. Let's see what is down there."

Geril nodded. "Agreed," he replied. *But we'll be back soon*, he thought.

Juna stepped past the dwarf and made her way through the door, pausing just above the first step, holding the lantern high. Geril turned to Thrag, "Stay here and guard the door," he said. "If we do not return, go to Balgavarr and tell Caulte that I have failed."

Thrag growled his disapproval with the idea. He jabbed Geril in the chest with a sharp talon. "I go," he rumbled.

Geril shook his head. "Please stay here," he asked. "I don't know how much room there is down there, and we may need room to maneuver. Your size may hinder us in combat." He unslung his axe as Thrag sagged with acceptance. "Good fellow. I won't be gone long." The devastator moved away and found a clear spot on the floor near the doorway. Crouching low onto his haunches, he became as still as the stone of the wall, his dark coat rendering him almost invisible, hidden among the shadows.

Satisfied that Thrag could take care of himself, Geril gripped the handle of his axe and followed Juna through the door. Once down out of sight of the temple, Juna opened the lantern to its fullest and bright light flooded the narrow confines of the staircase. They moved as quickly as they could and soon Geril was panting to keep up with his taller companion. Juna's long legs were constantly outdistancing him, and he was too proud to complain. He lost count of the stairs after two hundred and the number of turns and short passages after twenty. By his guess they had descended at least a full measure underground. The smooth worked walls were replaced by rough-hewn rock that echoed every step. The temperature had dropped steadily as they moved further down. Geril did not fail to notice the mirrorstones set at intervals along the walls. His suspicion of their purpose grew stronger.

At last the stairs ended. The light of the lantern revealed a long and narrow corridor stretching into darkness. Juna glanced down at the dwarf. "I hate this," she whispered. "How do your people live in such places?"

"Visit Balgavarr someday," he said. "It's nothing like this." He hugged himself and rubbed his arms vigorously. "I don't like it either, but we've come this far. Let's finish it. The sooner we find the relics, the sooner we can get out of here."

They walked quickly down the corridor, the wispy streams of their breath hanging in the cold air. Geril almost had to run to keep up with Juna's long strides and nearly ran into her when she stopped abruptly. "Damnation," she breathed, standing before a stone tablet that looked to have grown out of the floor. "What next?" The vaghan nudged her out of the way and muttered his own curse.

The corridor branched in four directions. There was no way to know which path to take. He turned to the tablet. It stood as tall as he was and was covered with runes. "Well, at least I know we're getting close," he said. "This is Magespeak, the language of the vaghan wizards' guild."

"Can you read it?"

"A little. Part of it says that this is the Maze of Ages. This other part reads, 'be led by light or shadowlost, ward the path at any cost, the way fades.' The rest I can't make out."

"Wonderful. The Maze of Ages. I've heard about this place, but I never thought it was real. We could get lost forever in that maze. Now what do we do?" Juna leaned against the wall. She glared at the grin on Geril's face.

"What is so amusing?"

Geril continued to smile as he pointed to the crystal mounted on the top of the tablet. "I know how to find out which way to take, but we don't have much time. I know what needs to be done, but we both can't go. You'll need to return to the temple."

"Why?" she asked, completely perplexed by his words.

"So you can turn on the lights."

# PART 7

*Some have claimed the inherent good in all races, but I
say to you that the darkened heart will never know the light.*
*—Tal the Righteous, Book of the Land 562 FA*

Juna raced back up the stairs from the catacombs to the
temple far above. She clutched the lantern in one hand and held
the other out to catch herself in case she lost her footing. *Had
there been this many steps on the way down?* She ran up them
until her leg muscles ached and her lungs burned. A sharp stitch
had developed in her side, but she dared not slow her pace. How
Geril could wait for her in the darkness she could not imagine.
Without the lantern, she knew the darkness would be absolute
and impenetrable. If she had been the one to wait, the fear would
have overwhelmed her in a very short time, but Geril had looked
unconcerned. "Just be quick, and get there before sunrise," he
had said.

He'd also told her to be sure to explain to Thrag that he
was alright, and have him remain in the temple until they
returned or the enemy discovered him. The other instructions
Geril had given her seemed unbelievable. He had a way to light
the entirety of the catacombs and the way to the Magestorm relics
at the same time? Were the vagha so clever? If what he had told
her was true, then much had been left out of the old legends of
the Magestorm.

She stumbled out of the doorway into the temple before
she realized where she was. She looked about in confusion for a
moment, as if not believing she had reached the surface. Hastily
she began to lower the wick on her lantern. They had come too
far to be discovered now. Then she was knocked off her feet by a
solid blow to her back from behind. The lantern went out as she
hit the floor, plunging the temple into darkness again.

A heavy form crouched over her and cold breath wafted over her neck.

"It's me, Thrag!" she gasped, barely able to draw a breath. "Get off me, you big brute." There was a moment of hesitation before Thrag moved away. He crouched down and stared at her with his glowing red eyes. "Geril?" he growled.

"Waiting below," she answered. "He needs our help. We have to find a lever around here somewhere." The eyes narrowed and she placed her hand on the hilt of the stolen sword she wore. If Thrag chose not to believe her, then she was in serious danger. The devastator could see in the dark, and the light spilling in from the bonfire in the courtyard was not enough for her to fight by.

"Lev-ver?" Thrag's eyes roamed over the interior of the temple.

Sighing her relief, the trooper let go of the sword and moved closer. "A stick," she said. "Coming out of the floor or the wall. Like what you opened the tunnel door with, remember?"

Thrag nodded. "Lev-ver is there," he said, pointing to the altar.

"Oh no," Juna moaned as she stared at the heaps of reeking dung piled on and around the altar. It would take time to dig through the mess, and time was something they had precious little of. Already she could see better. The darkness outside was turning a shade of gray as the sun began to rise. "I'm going to kill him. He knew exactly where it was." Still, she wasn't sure she would have preferred the overpowering darkness to plunging her hands into this foul muck. She stepped closer and was prepared to thrust her hands into the fetid mess when Thrag pulled her back. She didn't resist. Anything to keep from doing what she had been about to do.

The devastator stepped in front of her and held out his hands, palms out. The air in front of him sparkled as ice crystals materialized from nowhere. Instead of forming into the spears that Geril had described to her, they continued to amass before his hands. Thrag's breathing was faster and his entire body trembled as if he were exerting great force. Juna stepped back, suddenly fearful of what was about to happen.

A cold breeze swept through the temple as Thrag focused his might into the swirling balls of ice that had become maelstroms of frost larger than she was. Thrag grunted as he released the freezing orbs. With a whisper like a miniature blizzard, the orbs shot from his hands and impacted the mound of filth. Crackles filled the sanctum as the mound froze solid in an instant.

Almost immediately the smell lessened. Thrag was panting as he stepped back and slumped. Wearily he lifted his hand and pointed at her sword and then the frozen mound. Nodding that she understood, she drew the poniard and struck the mountain of frozen manure with all her strength.

It shattered, falling in frigid clumps to the floor. She expected there to be noise, but the avalanche was almost silent other than a dull thudding that she felt more than heard. The light from outside was stronger now. The temple door faced due east and the sun was just starting to crest over the city.

The altar was free of dung. A stained velvet curtain hung across the back of it. With a single stroke she sliced it away, revealing a surprisingly large opening for the small thing within.

There it was. In the hollow she found a single iron rod capped with a carved ball of polished aldehnwood that shone even in the pale light of dawn.

Wasting no time, she grabbed hold and pulled.

Nothing. The damned thing would not move. She threw down the sword and used both hands. Still it wouldn't budge. She cursed and was about to give another jerk when a hairy hand closed over both of hers. "Now," Thrag said in a low voice. Both of them pulled.

With a creak, the lever moved. The floor trembled and began to vibrate beneath their feet. The altar began to rise. Juna covered her mouth and gasped when she saw that the altar rested on a base that had been covered in sunstone. Almost immediately the reflective surface began to glow with the increasing light from the sun.

With a loud snap, the altar stopped moving when the top of the mirrored foundation was level with the top of her head. "I think we should get back and not look at this," she said, grabbing Thrag's arm and pulling him back.

The sun rose and bright golden light streamed through the door. The sunstone exploded with a radiance that made the sunlight seem pale in comparison. Both of them shielded their eyes. Turning away from the brilliance, Juna saw that the temple was filled with beams of iridescent light.

The brightest of them shone from the eyes carved over the door. As the sunstone glowed brighter, twin lances of luminescence flared from the eyes and impacted the single stone set in the wall across from the mouth. The lances were combined and reflected into the doorway. The sunstone inside the door seemed to burst into shimmering flame as more beams of light were reflected down the stairs. The selumari trooper stared wide-eyed in wonder.

"Those crafty little people," she whispered.

The inside of the temple was brighter than midday, but Juna could see that it would not last long. The sun would continue its daily trek into the sky, and once past the door of the temple the light would vanish as quickly as it had appeared. She grabbed the lantern and ran to the door. "Stay here, Thrag!" she said. "Guard us!" She raced down the stairs.

Geril sat alone in the dark. Sitting with his back against the cold stone of the wall, he tried to keep the utter darkness from seeping strength from his courage. He had tried several times to see anything, but even waving his hand in front of his eyes did no good. The blackness was thick and absolute. Being a dwarf, he was accustomed to being underground, and even to traveling in the dark of the vaghan mines, but this was by far the longest amount of time he had faced such a thick darkness alone.

While he waited, he found his pouch and removed the sightstone.

Holding the stone in his hand and concentrating produced only a dull red glow that barely lit up the area around him. Aside from little illumination, it made his skin appear as if it was covered in blood, so he quickly put it away.

He wondered how long Juna had been gone, and if she would find the lever that would light his path. He was counting on his suspicion that the temple had been built to disguise the hiding place of the Magestorm relics. With luck, the placement of the sunstones in the temple and the stairway meant that vaghan ingenuity and skill had constructed the entirety of the maze and the temple over it.

Eventually he could no longer tell if his eyes were open or closed, and he found himself growing sleepy. How long had it been since he had slept a night through? The last full night of sleep he could remember had been spent in the icy home of the frostwings. With all that had been happening, there had been little time for rest. Now that he'd stopped moving and thinking his body was crying out for him to stop. He fought it, knowing that any moment might find the maze alight with the bright rays of the faraway sun. Yet no matter how much he struggled against it, eventually sleep won over, and the dwarf's head fell forward onto his chest.

The floor shaking woke him from the depths of a sound sleep almost in an instant. He jerked awake and looked around wildly, bewildered for a moment to find himself unable to see. The entire catacomb was quaking, and he covered his mouth as dust fell from the ceiling. What was going on?

A brilliant beam of golden light filled the corridor, searing his eyes and making him cry out in surprise. As he had thought, the ray of light struck the crystal on the stone tablet and became even brighter as it was reflected down the second corridor on the left. With a shout of triumph he was on his feet and racing past the tablet. He understood more fully now the carved words on the stone. *The way fades*, it had read. He knew that as the sun rose beyond the doors of the temple, the light would go out. If he had not found the relics before then, he would be hopelessly lost in the maze. He ran as fast as he could, wishing for the first time in his life for limbs longer than his short vaghan legs. As a precaution, he drew his dagger and scored the walls as he dashed along.

There were many twists and turns, each one guided by a sunstone placed in the wall that reflected the light down the correct path. He had no time to marvel at the genius of the design; the light was already less bright than it had been when it first appeared. He was running out of time. His side was in agony as he rounded a turn and ran solidly into a dead end.

The impact flung him backwards, and he fell to the hard stone floor.

When the stars cleared, he lifted himself up with a groan and gasped for the breath that had been driven from his lungs. What had gone wrong? He had been so sure he would be led right to the treasure. He glared at the wall that had had the audacity to be in his way, and his eyes went wide.

Engraved into the wall was the open hand symbol of the cantrip, the sign of battle magic. The beam of light fell upon it, and it was radiating warmth and glory in a million colorful rainbows on the walls, floor, and ceiling. Carved stone wasn't supposed to sparkle like that. He stepped closer and gasped. The inside of the mark was filled with diamonds, a king's treasure worth of them.

He recalled the riddle. What was next? The Maze of Ages had been the sign of the second, which was his own race of the vagha. The sun had worked its will and the maze was alight with that power. *Then play the mage—a wave of fear, a power quickly summoned here.* Apparently he was going to have to use magic of some sort, but what kind? He was an untrained user of what little Latkis had taught him. If great power was needed, they were in deep trouble. Carefully, he approached the wall. The ray of light was warm as he cautiously laid his hand on the carving. It was a perfect match.

Magic flooded into him. More power than he had ever imagined filled him, body and soul. What was the source of this magical energy, and what was he supposed to do with it? Was it the sunlight? Did the magic come from the power of the morning sun directed from far away into darkness? *If open maw you wish to see, the word unspoken is the key.* He cursed the cryptic words of the riddle. What did it mean by a word unspoken?

The light was fading quickly, and the darkness was closing in. If he didn't get this open soon… There was a loud cracking and dust filled the air.

He looked up to see a fissure in the stone. Understanding suddenly flooded through his mind. The answer to the riddle was hidden within the very words.

The word unspoken.

He smiled. Closing his eyes, he allowed the magic to fill him. He imagined a door swinging open, the picture in his mind clear and unclouded.

*Open,* he thought. *Open.*

The fissure widened and began to spread. Foul air, sealed away for a more than two centuries, hissed out. He choked and gagged but kept his hand firmly on the symbol until it crumbled away. The diamonds disintegrated with puffs of warmth. Large chunks of rock fell around him, but none touched him. The magic shielded him from harm as the barrier fell with a crash. The last of the light streaked past him and struck a gem mounted on a pedestal inside the chamber he had opened. A small star began to shine inside the immense room, and as the beam that had guided him faded away it continued to shine brightly.

The council chamber of Balgavarr was puny in comparison to the room he entered. It yawned wide and tall as his home's city market. Racks and stands displayed fine weapons and shields, though they lay under a thick coating of dust. Tables kiltered under the weight of decay, but still held smaller tools of arcane craftsmanship.

He moved slowly, stepping over broken stone and staring in wonder at the vast array of dust-covered remnants from a long-ago war.

They lay everywhere in neat piles. Some were stationed on stone tables carved from the rock walls and others in heaps on the very floor. His eyes fell on innumerable relics of every type of magic, sorted by the elemental power they were made imbued with. His eyes picked out a quiver of sky blue arrows and a bow of the same hue carved from ironwood. He had never thought to see the legendary arrows, and now his trembling hand caressed the various colored items. One or two of the famed missiles could fetch a hefty sum; here were entire bales of them, bundled and ready for battle.

His gaze found racks of vorpal swords and more. Beyond the racks stood row upon row of spiked blade golems, bristling with knives and swords. In awe, he beheld countless dragonstaffs leaning against the tall and numerous columns of stone throughout the chamber. There was more magical might in this chamber than he could have imagined in a dozen lifetimes.

He knelt near a group of massive gilt chests and lifted the lid of the closest one. Inside were more than a dozen jeweled rings of stars, and in the next he found the most desired objects of the magic users of Esfah. With reverence he lifted a golden magi's crown. In his hands he held an object that could allow even the most inexperienced theurgist to channel the forces of the world's heart with ease. A wizard wearing this crown would be almost unstoppable. The headpiece was beautiful: a work of true craftsmanship. Forged by the hands of the gremmlobahnd and tempered with the magic of the earth, small jewels of every type lined the whole of the crown. Such items were priceless. Only the gnomes knew the secrets to crafting such powerful artifacts, interweaving their construction with the mythic star metal, the eldrymetallum.

It was no wonder Matrek wanted this treasure for his people. With such an arsenal, the morehl would be obliterated. For a moment the young dwarf was tempted to save what he had found. Balgavarr and Tulgesh would be saved for all time, and the people of Nature would be the rulers of this region of Esfah. Yet his father had taught him that ultimate power ultimately corrupts. The world was better off without these things. In the hands of a leader with a darkened heart, the potential for evil was too risky.

Geril stood up, still holding the crown. Now how was he to seal the relics away forever? Was it possible to bring down the ceiling and bury them away, and how could he do such a thing?

He was still considering what to do when the keen edge of a sword blade touched his neck. "Well done, little one," a voice said. "My Lord will be pleased. My thanks for marking your path. It made finding you so much simpler."

Chills went down his spine. He knew the voice, but it had changed. It was thicker and nefarious. "Juna? What are you doing?" Slowly he turned around to face her.

"Doing? I am recovering what has been lost for far too long."

"So, you betray me to Matrek?"

She smirked. "Matrek? Ha! He is finished. With these relics the morehl will finish what's left of Matrek's resistance and open the doors to Balgavarr. This petty war is finished."

Geril gasped. "You would betray your own race?"

She pressed the blade against his throat, drawing a line of blood. "My race?" She threw back her head and laughed. "You foolish little imp! My race will rule Esfah, and whatever is left of yours will serve us."

"But… you are selumari," he said, not wanting to believe what he was hearing. "You are a child of Nature."

She spat. "Child of Nature? A convincing performance, don't you think? I even made you believe I was appalled by the damage to the city and the temple. I am no selumari. Neither am I morehl, but the children of Lord Death took me in. I am frehlasuhl, the grey elves that some call the mudbloods." She laughed at his dumbfounded expression. "You thought I was putting on a disguise to look like a morehl, didn't you? At no point was my skin truly blue. Don't you realize now that I am a master infiltrator? A necessary skill of my kind, since races of every stripe and elves of every color have made it their mission to wipe out my hybrid race."

Geril shook his head. "Your eyes," he whispered. "Your eyes are blue."

"Amusing, isn't it? My father was a selumari who dared take a lava elf for his mate. After I was born she killed him while he slept and brought me to her people, where I was raised to hate everything born of Nature. Lord Laman thought my unfortunate heritage would be useful some day. Now his words have proven true."

She flicked her eyelids shut and open again, this time her eyes were black. Juna did it again; they were white this time—some trick of frehlasuhl race.

Geril lowered his eyes and stared at the floor. "It can't be true," he whispered. "It can't be."

"It is true," she said, "but enough of this, discuss it with my Lord Death!" She raised the sword to strike.

The vaghan moved faster than she thought possible for a being so compact in size. His arm came up and the sword bounced off the magi's crown with a cascade of sparks. She cried out as the impact stung her hand and she nearly dropped the poniard. He ducked under her next swing and leaped over the chests. Juna advanced on him, the sword in her hand trembling. She sneered at him. "You prolong the inevitable. You've nowhere to run."

Geril retreated, his eyes searching wildly for anything to fight with. His heart ached in his chest and fear clutched at him. She had spoken truly; there was nowhere to go. Juna's betrayal wounded him far more than any weapon.

Words spoken by Caulte in the home of the frostwings reoccurred to him, words of how a selumari speaking lies had lulled the amazons and feral into complacency. The lies that had lost the golden plains of Seshara to the morehl.

"You," he hissed. "You betrayed them all. The feral. The amazons. You were the one that came to them. You cost them their home."

Her smile was pure malevolence. "You're quick, dwarf. That was another of Laman's ideas that gave us a victory where we might have tasted defeat. It may even gain us Balgavarr." She moved closer. "Who else but a selumari ally could get inside and open wide the doors to an unbreachable mountain?" Her eyes found a rack of vorpal swords and she cast aside the poniard and grabbed the handle of the more powerful weapon, a sword imprinted with Death runes. It hummed in her hands, eager for battle and bloodshed.

Geril gasped. Typically, to use a blade devoted to Death as anything other than a normal sword, its user had to be fully devoted to the Death god.

He knew his time grew shorter by the second; he could not avoid her for much longer. Fear was rising within him. Not for himself, but for the vagha and all the races of Nature. He had shown her secrets of his race that could be their undoing. He reached for the axe strapped to his back and realized he still held the crown. An impossible idea quickly formed. He placed the crown on his head. At first it was loose and he held it in place, but suddenly the crown shrank until it fit perfectly. Surprised and suddenly eager, he closed his eyes and sought the magic of the earth.

When he opened them again Juna had come much closer, and the air in front of him swarmed with golden motes of magic. She had seen his movement and had recognized the object he now wore. Her steps were cautious. He swept his arm up and grabbed a handful of the motes. Never before had he held so much power. His hand shook from the vibration of magical energy.

"Whatever you're planning won't work, vaghan. I'll take your head before you can cast a spell."

"I don't think so," Geril said scornfully, and opened his hand. The motes had transformed into a sphere of damp soil. He threw the handful of mud down onto the floor of the cavern. With all his strength he leaped for the closest carved shelf. He landed hard on a pile of enchanted arrows, nearly bashing his head open against the wall and cutting his arm on an arrowhead. He looked back to see what his hastily cast spell had done.

The floor bucked and warped like boiling magma. Juna waved her arms in a desperate attempt to keep her balance. The mud spread rapidly, and the firm rock was changing, becoming soft and liquid. In the space of seconds the floor became a bubbling cauldron of mud; the entire cavern shifted with impending doom. Tables and all, the relics began to sink beneath the mire.

Geril quickly tossed the magic arrows into the sludge where they sank from sight. Racks holding staffs and swords vanished beneath the surface. Juna screamed in frustration as the last of the items slipped from sight. And then she noticed that she herself was sinking. She screamed again, this time in fear. "Geril!" she cried, dropping the vorpal sword.

The mud sucked her down to her thighs. "Please!" she shrieked. "I don't want to die!"

Geril watched dispassionately as the mud crept up to her chest. "The evil of your kind must be infectious," he said quietly, "because I don't care if you do."

The mud was now up to her neck and she wailed. The scream echoed off the walls and Geril sighed, resisting the urge to try to help her. She took one last desperate breath as her head sank beneath the surface. Her uplifted hand clawed at the air before it slipped from sight into the churning earth.

Taking the crown from his head, he looked at it for a moment. Here was a key to great power for any who possessed it. The temptation to keep it for his own was strong. It could do so much for him and his people. It would help drive the morehl from the Kafnysan Mountains forever and bring glory to the vagha and peace to this remote region of Esfah. He could rule all of… With a snarl he cast the relic away. The mud swallowed it without so much as a gurgle. Now he understood the evil that the Magestorm items had brought to Esfah. Shudders racked him as he realized how close he had come to succumbing to that power.

Moments passed, and he wondered if he was going to spend the rest of his life on this stone bench. With the sound of footsteps on gravel, the floor began to firm up again as he watched. Crackling and rumbling, it transformed again into solid rock. Not trusting his eyes, he carefully lowered himself from the bench. His boots did not sink. The spell had faded.

Looking around, he saw that the once full chamber was now empty of all magic items. Even the mighty golems and mantlets and had sunk away.

This secret cache of relics from the Magestorm War were gone forever. Even if someone were to discover what had happened, it would take years of difficult digging to uncover them. Geril knew he would take this secret with him to the grave.

The light from the crystal flickered. The pedestal was canted at an angle, but had not sunk. The crystal was dimming, the illumination sputtering like a candle flame in the breeze. When it went out, he would be plunged back into darkness.

A dull glow caught his eye. Juna's lantern sat near the crumbled entry, set there as she crept up behind him with sword drawn. He had his way out.

With the lantern he could follow his own marks back to the main corridor, and from there to the surface. With any luck, Thrag and their early morning workings in the temple remained undiscovered. The floor was no longer the smooth worked surface it had been. Now it was covered with ripples and bumps that made footing treacherous, but his feet knew rock and his steps were sure.

The score of his dagger was still evident on the wall. It was hard to see in the dim light of the lantern, but it was enough to guide him. Once back in the main corridor, he made his way as fast as his weariness would allow to the steps. Far above the countless steps, Thrag waited for him. Half of his purpose in Tulgesh was finished. Now if he and Thrag could somehow sneak back out of the city… He swallowed hard. Just the two of them now. Juna's betrayal and death hurt more than he cared to admit, even to himself. War did this. Would there ever be a time when the races of Esfah could live together in peace?

With one heavy sigh at the futility of wishful thinking, he ran up the stairs.

Taran stepped from the broken doors of the temple and emerged into bright morning sunlight. Already the air was hot and moist from the nearby sea. Soon they would leave this wretched place far behind. The Kafnysan mountain range was cold, but at least it was dry.

His wyvern was tethered near the remains of the gate, feeding from a dripping bowl held by a young selumari slave-girl. The female grimaced with every bleeding mouthful his mount took. Blood had spattered on her face and clothes, and Taran chuckled. If the bowl of meat wasn't enough to sate the wyvern's hunger, the girl might serve another purpose.

He checked the reins and straps holding the small leather saddle. The scabbard and holster were secure, as were the weapons they held. His pouch of blast powder and iron balls was also fastened tight and within easy reach during flight. Everything was ready.

The reptilian steed jerked its head and screeched. He patted the scaly neck. "Easy, girl," he cooed. "We'll be leaving soon."

Not soon enough for him and the rest of his squad. Bunking in the temple was doing no good for the morale of the riders. The rooms were damp and uncomfortable, and the atmosphere wholly unpleasant for morehl. Some of his squad were convinced that the place was haunted. Why, just this morning many were talking in hushed tones of the strange occurrences that had happened during the night. The dung that had been piled around the altar had mysteriously fallen and scattered throughout the temple, leaving the altar completely uncovered. Some were claiming it was the work of angry spirits.

Bueron was quick to quash such talk. He had been certain his defilement of the holy place would earn him recognition from Laman or Emperor Saugor.

The conqueror had not seemed impressed, and the king was a long way from hearing of anything.

Taran was one of only a few that had not thought it wise to destroy a holy place. While most of his race sneered at the idea of higher beings other than Lord Death, he knew that most legends usually had some basis in fact. If there were gods of Nature, he thought it best not to anger them. However, this opinion would quickly gain him a slit throat if it were known. He was glad the army was moving out of the city. The strangeness of the lowlands was disconcerting. Once they controlled Balgavarr, he would warm himself by the lava streams and burn away the chill that these lower climes had settled in his bones.

Taking the reins in hand, he climbed to the saddle as Bueron walked from the temple with a swagger of arrogance that set Taran's teeth to grinding. He despised the egotism of the commander, but forced his irritation down before it showed on his face. Bueron practically strutted across the courtyard to his mount. He jerked the reins from the hands of the slave as he settled into the saddle.

He whistled shrilly, calling all to attention. "The main force has already begun the march to Balgavarr. We will overtake them and scout ahead. If we encounter resistance, we are to eliminate it." Cheers sounded through the courtyard, and Taran forced himself to join in. "Let the riders lead the way to victory!" More cheers, but this time Taran didn't join in. Wrapped in a blanket of conceit, Bueron failed to notice.

Bueron pulled his pistol and cocked back the hammer. The slave that had been caring for his wyvern looked up with an expression of resigned sorrow on his face. The commander pulled the trigger and laughed in satisfaction as the back of the slave's head exploded out in a spray of green blood and chunks of bone. The rest of the riders quickly followed his example and executed the remaining slaves. The elf girl that had been feeding his mount looked up at him without fear. He was impressed with her bravery in the way she faced Lord Death. He glanced at the open doors to the temple and wondered if there was a horrible price for shedding innocent blood in a holy place. He leaned down.

"I have no wish to kill you without cause," he whispered. He looked around quickly to make sure no one was watching him. "You have cared for my wyvern despite your feelings. When I fire my pistol, fall down. I spare your life." He took out his weapon and shot into the ground between her feet. When the smoke cleared she lay crumpled on the ground, but he could see her breathing. So she lived.

He'd spared her life, but for how long? With Tulgesh in ruins, her lifespan would be measured in days. Still, he felt some small satisfaction at having shown mercy. Why was that? With few exceptions, the morehl did not know mercy. He shrugged the discomforting thoughts aside.

Wyverns shrieked as Bueron led the ascent into the sky. As one of the officers, Taran was next in the air. From high above the towers, he could see the last remnants of the departing army just visible in the distance as they marched toward the far distant mountain range. The trogs would be leading the march under the close supervision of morehl officers. The first losses of the battle would be theirs. The dwarves would fight ferociously against the goblins, as their hatred for the swamp dwellers would drive them into a frenzy. The army would likely lose most of the trog forces, but the vagha would be bloodied and exhausted from the battle. They would then be easy pickings for the still fresh morehl soldiers. The fight would be brief, and the city theirs.

The wyverns were all aloft and glided into formation as the beasts snorted and cried their ear-piercing shrieks. Taking his reserved position just behind and to Bueron's right, Taran settled in for the long flight. The city fell behind as they began to overtake the heavy troops at the rear of the army.

Two days would see them in the foothills, where it was expected the dwarves would show the first resistance.

Three days would see the final victory of the morehl, and his rise to power as commander of the wyvern riders – one way or another.

When destiny calls, it is best to answer.

The temple was eerily silent. From far above the floor, Geril and Thrag waited to be sure that no one remained who might discover them. They had watched with apprehension as the last of the riders and then the commander left the building. Geril sat cross-legged on the wide rafter and tried not to think about how far he was from the floor. Thrag acted as if he was unaware of how high they were by actually yawning. Geril shook his head and sighed.

Thrag had grabbed him as soon as he had appeared in the door and clamped one huge hand over his mouth to stifle the cry of alarm that the dwarf almost uttered. He then pulled him back into the shadows, his leathery black wings wrapping around them and further concealing the pair.

Geril was soon gasping as the air quickly grew stale. At least he wasn't hot as Thrag put off very little body heat, but the wait was agony. It felt like hours had passed before Thrag's wings opened and Geril gasped fresh air.

Before he could say anything Thrag had grabbed him under the arms and leapt for the ceiling.

The beam was two full paces wide, allowing Geril to sit comfortably without fear of falling off, but the layer of dust was years thick and bothered his nose. To avoid raising choking clouds he had to sit completely still, which was difficult and tiring. He yawned and prayed that they would be able to leave soon.

The sounds of the wyverns in the courtyard had grown silent some time ago. They had heard shots and both had jumped, then the flapping of wings as the wyverns took flight. Silence descended over the temple like a thick blanket. The vaghan and the areosan waited for more than an hour to make sure that the temple was deserted. Thrag stretched his wings and sniffed the air. "Gone," he growled, his red eyes glowing faintly in the dimness.

Geril stood and stretched the kinks out of his legs. His joints popped loudly from having sat for so long in one position. "Are you certain? I'd hate for us to be discovered by leaving too early."

Thrag nodded. "Gone," he said again. The devastator gently lifted Geril and spread his wings. Stepping off the beam, they floated smoothly to the floor. Cautiously he made his way to the door and looked out. The outer courtyard was deserted save for the bodies of more than a dozen selumari that lay scattered around the wall. The only sign of life was a lone girl cradling a body. Stepping into the sunlight, the pair approached her. She cringed as she looked over her shoulder. Seeing a dwarf and a creature unlike any she had ever known elicited only a small gasp. Geril touched her shoulder. "We are friends," he said.

She nodded and turned her eyes to the still face of the corpse. "He was my brother," she choked as tears fell on the pale cheeks. "There was no need to kill any of us. We were no threat." She looked up at him again. "Why do they hate us?"

"It is their nature," Geril replied, crouching down. "Their black hearts are filled with the hatred and animosity of Lord Death for all things hale and good. I think that only when they destroy all that is born of Nature will the morehl find their own peace."

"I want them all dead," she moaned. "Am I wrong to want them all to die?"

Geril shook his head. "There are many that share that wish. If only wishing could make it so."

"They have left for Balgavarr, I heard them say so. Is that where you are going?"

"Soon enough. Thrag can get us there in less than a day, so if we leave too soon we will overtake them. First, we must go to Deepmire."

"The swamps? Why?"

He stood up. "I cannot say because I'm not quite sure myself. Most of the morehl are leaving the city, but you should hide until they are gone. Many of your people are hiding in the ironwood forest. I think you should go there until it is safe to return to Tulgesh."

She nodded. "I will bury my brother and the others first," she said. "Perhaps here in the earth of the temple they will find peace. I would ask you to help me, but from your face I can see that whatever takes you to Deepmire is urgent. Be wary of the swamps, friend dwarf. There are dangers there still unknown to us."

Geril nodded and turned away. Thrag lifted him to his broad shoulders.

"That's what I'm afraid of," he said as they took to the sky.

Deepmire was two days from Tulgesh by foot, a day by horse, and only a few hours by wing. Thrag flew unerringly toward where the wetlands glistened like a million emeralds on the horizon. Before he could grow tired of the flight, they had been over the swamps. Sunlight flashed brightly in the countless pools that passed by below. Geril groaned. He hated getting wet.

"Take us down anywhere, Thrag," he'd said. "It doesn't matter where we start looking, I guess."

Two days had passed in damp misery. It didn't help matters that he had no idea what he was looking for. What could Caulte have sensed here? There was nothing but wet and more wet. Everything was covered with a sheen of moisture. The wood he managed to scrounge was soaked and refused his best efforts to light it with flint and steel. Not that he needed a fire. The nights were almost as hot as the day, and the humidity made it all the worse. At least food had been plentiful. Thrag caught small fish, and the trees were laden with large sweet fruit.

He had decided to stay only two days, and then they would fly as fast as possible to Balgavarr. It was now approaching midday of their second in Deepmire. Whatever Caulte believed was here was not going to show itself.

The mystery, such as it was; would remain unsolved. Resting in the shade of an unfamiliar type of tree, he stroked the haft of his axe idly and wondered how close the morehl were to Balgavarr. Thrag was scratching at the ground restlessly. Geril's eyes drooped. The heat was making him sleepy.

A loud snarl pulled him from sleep. Looking about, he saw Thrag standing erect and ice spears forming in each hand. Long fangs were bared and the growl frightening. Grabbing his axe, he jumped to his feet and stood beside the devastator. "What is it?"

That was when he heard the rustling of leaves and the soft lapping of water. Sinewy shapes moved between the thick trunks and the low bushy plants. Thrag roared and flung a spear. Something hissed and a dark shape splashed into a pool of water. Another spear was already forming, the ice crackling as it took shape.

The forms moved in closer, and now he could see the long, slender bodies that looked like nightmares come to life. Whatever they were, their intentions were clear by the wickedly sharp and curving blades many of them carried. They slithered in from all directions, surrounding the pair. Thrag launched more spears and most of the rapidly swimming creatures dodged easily, but one of the larger ones fell, skewered. With a hiss, it splashed into the water. With eyes wide with fear, Geril backed until he was standing close to his friend. He held the haft of his axe in a death-grip, knuckles white.

Two of the snake things darted in from either side, one with a sword held high in a twisted tentacle. Geril ducked the swipe and swung his axe.

Greenish-black blood flew in a spray as the heavy blade sliced through scaled flesh. The creature shrieked and toppled over. Thrag grabbed the second by both of its snakelike appendages. Muscles bulged and he let out a rasping grunt as he pulled both arms from the torso. Others behind them moved back a few paces.

Geril stole a quick glance at the dead thing at his feet. The features were distorted, but he clearly recognized the sharp angled facial structure of a coral elf. The one Thrag had killed had evidently once been a trog. The large goblin nose and brow ridges were unmistakable. Looking at the others that still moved slowly around them, he saw that most had been coral elves, but there were also a few morehl and even a small number of the ghwereste.

Something had caused them to mutate, change into these things that now faced them. Their voices were soft whispers that seemed to echo in his ears. *–Take them – make them a part of us – 'ware their weapons.*

Several of the fiends produced vials from the pouches at their hips. Whatever the murky substance was in those corked, glass ampoules could not be ascertained.

Another of them glided in, thrusting with the point of its blade. Thrag shoved Geril out of the way, but the blade still scored the dwarf's side. Geril cried out and swung his axe in a clumsy arc that his attacker evaded. The axe cut nothing but air. Geril saw the sword that was about to take off his head. The creature hissed in triumph.

Thrag got there first. His large hand caught the scaled wrist of Geril's attacker and he wrenched the slender being toward him. Talons flashed as his claws ripped away the throat. It dropped like a stone. Its other arm did not end in a fist but a snake's head. The writhing serpent attached at its shoulder. Before Thrag could evade the strike, the head snapped forward and sank dripping fangs into the side of the areosan.

Thrag bellowed as the reptilian warrior splashed the wound with the gray waste-water from its bottle. One of the others hissed, "The waters of Lethial!"

Grabbing the snake, he ripped it from the body and threw it far into the trees before slumping. Geril positioned himself in front of his friend and brandished his axe. "Get back!" he shouted. The snake-things retreated, but only out of striking range of the half-moon blade. A low hum filled the air as they began to sway in unison. Geril was stunned. What were they doing? He risked a glance over his shoulder at Thrag and gasped at what he saw.

Thrag's side was glowing with a sickly bright green around the two puncture wounds. The frostwing was panting hoarsely and groaning. He fell over onto his side. The glow was spreading, and as it did, the blue-black hair turned gray and fell out, leaving bare skin which looked to be forming scales. Geril whirled around to the creatures. "What did you do to him?" he cried.

*–Make it ours–*

"Eldurim's blood, no," he said. Not caring for his own safety, he lowered his axe and turned to Thrag. The devastator was growing weaker. Even his dark eyes now pulsed with the same ill glow. "Fight it, Thrag. Don't become one of them."

Thrag looked up and met Geril's eyes. In them Geril saw a fierce determination that swallowed and overcame the glow. Lifting his hand, Thrag extended his claws and slashed his side where the glow was strongest. Then he slowly got to his feet and growled.

Geril expected blood to drip from the four gashes in Thrag's side, but what did seep from the wounds was a thick green ooze that stank of rot and corruption. When it hit the soggy ground, it seemed to come alive and slither away. Geril gaped at the living poison, a poison that Thrag had managed to rid himself of.

The glow faded from the devastator's body, but the gashes from his own claws remained, seeping dark blood. Where scales had started to form the skin returned to normal, but slightly mottled in color. Thrag got to his feet.

Sinister hisses filled the area. Geril gripped his axe and prepared to fight, but felt two strong hands grasp his waist. Thick leathery wings swept out and down, lifting them from the ground.

The menacing cries of the creatures followed them. Looking down, Geril saw them rushing in from all sides to where the two of them had just been. As Thrag flew back towards Tulgesh, the attackers followed through the swamps, their lithe forms allowing them to move faster than any creature Geril had ever seen.

*They're stalking us. They've been stalking us for days,* he thought. *That's what they do. Stalk their prey and change them.* He recalled a vague entry on them in the *Book of the Land*; though he'd never seen a swamp stalker, he knew they were known as the sarslayan, and they were dangerous.

Nightfall found them well beyond Tulgesh among the ironwoods, but far from Matrek's hidden refuge. Geril doubted that the selumari champion would welcome him. Thrag was trembling as he lowered the dwarf to the earth. Considering what his mighty friend had gone through, he was amazed that he had brought them so far from the swamps. Thrag dropped into a deep sleep almost as soon as he stretched out.

Geril sat with his back against Thrag's uninjured side. Time was passing far too rapidly. In the days they had been exploring Deepmire, the morehl horde would have marched at least halfway to Balgavarr. The wyverns would reach his home first, and would most likely begin the assault.

The goblins would then follow soon after. The feral and frostwings would hopefully reach Balgavarr in time to meet the attack.

He realized he was bone-weary and closed his eyes. Before he fell asleep, he said a prayer that Thrag would be recovered enough by morning to fly.

Sleep claimed him.

# PART 8

*The tapestry of time is woven with threads of fate. The hands of destiny weave the pattern of the loom, and the ages of Esfah turn.*

*—Alrys Windsinger, The Cyrean Songs 948 SA*

Balgavarr waited. The main doors were closed, and all other ways into the mountain were either blocked or under guard. The scouts had returned with dire news of the approaching invasion. Trog thugs followed the cavalry mounted on dogs, wolves, and leopards. They had rapidly crossed the vast plains of Seshara from Tulgesh and were in the foothills. Within a day they would be close enough for the vagha to smell. Sentry lines had been set up and the city prepared for siege. Mothers and their children had been removed to the deepest part of the mines where the shafts joined tunnels that would take them into the remote forests of the Dur'sona, far to the north of Balgavarr. If the city fell, at least they would be safe.

Down the mountain from the city, crouched behind hastily constructed rock fortifications, the crossbowmen and marksmen readied their bolts. They would be the first to see conflict, and it was up to them to inflict heavy casualties on the trogs. The goblins were dangerous fighters up close, so the fewer that made it through the defensive line, the better.

Elder Vors made his way through the rock passageways, his staff clacking on the hard stone and sending echoes up and down the empty corridors. He carried a flickering torch that barely lit his way, but his eyesight was still sharp, and that was sufficient. Balgavarr felt empty, and the emptiness tore at him. Too much had gone wrong in the last few days. The discovery of Ghuren's body only a few stone throws from the city had cast a pall over the population. He had been dead too long for the spark of life to be re-awakened.

The Elder had been widely liked and respected. A hero of the city and the son of a legend, his murder both frightened and angered the inhabitants of the dwarf city. Vors dreaded what he would say to Geril if he returned from wherever he had gone. Many of the people blamed Vors for allowing Ghuren to walk outside unescorted. He owed that to Jeffon and Hergat. Those two had been quick to tell how he had told them to leave Ghuren to walk alone. If Geril were to learn that… well, it was widely known that the grandson of Zephras Thunderfist had inherited the temper of his father's father. Vors did not want to be on the receiving end of that anger.

Making his way to the upper levels, he inspected the battlements and the soldiers in position there. All of them wore their battle armor and watched the mountainside with sharp eyes that would notice the smallest creature daring to intrude on their home. As he passed, each of them lifted a fist to heart in salute. "Earth and fire, Elder," they said. To Vors' ears, the ancient gesture sounded hollow, and did nothing to lift his spirits. Still, he returned each salute and managed a smile. He spoke encouraging words that were forgotten as soon as they passed his lips.

He continued to climb until he reached the archaic stairs that would take him to the very top of Balgavarr Mountain. His old bones protested the climb, but he ignored the aches and started up.

The stairway was cold and full of dust that drifted up in clouds whenever he took a step. Taking each step carefully, he made his way up into darkness until the fresh air caressed his face. He stepped from between the hollow of two massive boulders and stood on the summit of Balgavarr Mountain. The sun was nearing midday.

From this great height he could just barely see the distant sea as a blue haze on the horizon. The plains spread out before the mountains like a golden blanket. The army of the morehl was fast approaching, and they were much closer than he had hoped. Only hours away now, they would enter the foothills no later than dusk of the following day. From there it would be a short march to the hidden city. Death would soon visit Balgavarr. It seemed that Geril's mission to seek the aid of the areosa had been for nought.

He turned away and stared at the circle of upright stones that crowned the summit. Placed by ancient hands unknown, many years ago, the granite slabs allowed the magic users to more easily focus their power. A wizard in this place could draw more magic from Esfah's heart than normal. Rannon and his guild would conjure spells from here when the battle began. Spells to give their warriors strength, defense, or speed to outmaneuver the enemy forces.

He had come here to escape the accusing eyes that seemed to be everywhere. Even the other Elders seemed to look upon him with disdain. It was almost too much.

He moved to the closest stone and placed his hand on the smooth surface. It hummed under his palm as he felt the traces of magic that had formed these monoliths centuries ago, this stone had been hewn and set in place by magic. "Eldurim preserve us," he whispered.

"That remains to be seen," Rannon's voice spoke from the cleft.

Vors turned as the leader of the Wizards' Guild stepped from between the rocks. Although not an Elder of the people or a member of the Council, Rannon sa'Arthun's voice was one that carried weight and was ignored by none. "Eldurim and his sister tend to let us find our own way. If he should turn his eyes upon us, he will do nothing to affect the outcome."

The wizard crooked his jaw, "Unless Eldurim or Firiel send their chosen Champion," he mumbled.

Vors gripped his staff until his fingers ached. "Why are you here? Have you come to blame me for Ghuren's death as others have?"

Rannon chuckled. "I have come to prepare for the rest of the guild. We shall do our part in defense of the city from here. As for blame, you put far more upon yourself than anyone else does. Most are thinking of the coming battle, not of you." Together they stared down at the plains. "Closer still. Our bowmen will face the goblins come sunrise tomorrow."

"It seems Ghuren's whelp has failed his quest. The areosa must have eaten him. He should have returned by now."

Rannon chuckled. "The boy has always rankled you, hasn't he, Vors? From his first breath, I think. Your dislike for his family has birthed suspicion of him, and you discount him too soon, I think. He will return to Balgavarr, and I believe he carries our salvation with him. Give up your hatred, Vors. It makes you weak, and we need our Elders strong."

"Your confidence in the descendant of the Thunderfist will be the undoing of us all, Rannon. Remember, it was I that told you that." He turned away angrily and strode to the rocks. He paused only to look back and glare at the wizard before he squeezed between the boulders and left Rannon alone on the mountaintop.

The wizard shook his head. "I will, Vors. I will."

Geril sat with his back against the hard bark of an ironwood and cursed.

Two days they had lost while Thrag recuperated. After escaping Deepmire they had flown to this small grove, near Tulgesh but far enough from Matrek's refugees to avoid an unpleasant confrontation with the champion.

After a night's rest he had been ready to fly home, but Thrag had been far too weak to travel.

The wound on the frostwing's side was ghastly. His self-inflicted gashes that had drained most of the poison were swollen and dripped blood and green ooze. Thrag lay panting on his side, his claws digging furrows in the rich soil. Occasionally he bared his fangs and growled long and low. His eyes shifted from black to green, then back to black. The bald spot on his side continually change from smooth skin into scales, which fell off when it became skin once more. Thrag's fight to remain unchanged was not over.

Geril did what he could, bringing his friend water from a nearby stream, and covering him with a blanket of leaves when night fell. He chafed at the delay, but worry for the frostwing was first in his mind. Should Thrag lose this battle, he would start his way home. Until then, he would remain by his side. He owed Thrag that much.

He woke on the morning of the third day with swords surrounding him.

"Not again," he muttered, rubbing his eyes. He knew without reaching for it that his axe was no longer by his side. The blades moved back as he sat up, but stayed ready to skewer him should he make a wrong move.

"You're getting careless, Geril," said a familiar voice.

He didn't bother to turn and face the speaker. "I'm tired, Matrek. I don't think I've ever been as bone-weary as I am now. Tell these lackeys of yours to move their swords and let me stand up."

Matrek lifted his hand and gave a light wave. The troopers moved back but did not put away their weapons. Geril stood, noticing that Thrag still lay sleeping nearby. The frostwing seemed to be resting soundly, so maybe he had beaten the poison. Beyond him, four giant golden eagles were tethered to a post driven into the ground. The huge raptors fluffed their feathers and lifted their wings a bit to catch the morning sunlight. That was how they had been spotted. "Where is Juna?" demanded the elf leader.

Geril thought quickly. "Juna? Wasn't she the soldier that brought me to you? I haven't seen her since then." Telling Matrek of Juna's treachery would gain him nothing and possibly raise the champion's anger that someone would dare question the loyalty of a selumari.

Confusion bloomed on the coral elf's features. "You have not seen her? She vanished just before you did. I guessed that you had abducted her as a prisoner of war."

"Our people are not at war, Matrek. I abducted nobody."

"Not at war? That remains to be seen. Your actions have made me wonder how much the vagha value our alliance, or whether it is still necessary."

Geril tried not to show his shock, but knew he failed. "The alliance has lasted more than a hundred years. Why would you break it? Why would your king do that?"

Matrek shook his head. "Our king is far away in Aurria across the sea. It's been two years since the last emissary visited. I doubt he even knows that Tulgesh is lost. Should he make an appearance, I'll be sure to bring him up to date. The peace between us is nothing to him, I can assure you that. Now tell me, what did you do with the relics of the Magestorm?"

There was no point in lying, Geril saw that. With the city mostly abandoned, the survivors had been free to enter the city without facing Death.

A selumari girl burying dead in the courtyard of the temple would have told of the dwarf leaving on the shoulders of an unknown creature. Matrek must have found the catacombs. Following his marks on the walls would have taken them to the chamber. Such a large dead end would have told Matrek all he needed to know. "They're gone," he said. "Gone forever."

"What did you do?" Matrek snarled.

"What I had to do." The dwarf brushed past the ring of troopers that surrounded him. "The evil of the relics is not what they do with magic, but rather how they change the heart of whoever uses them. Could you have resisted that call, Matrek? I almost did not. I could feel myself becoming hungry for power. I wanted to rule and use the magic of the relics to make myself a king." He lowered his gaze and shook his head. "Our world has enough sorrow in it. I could never forgive myself if another such storm were to be unleashed again because of my failure to do the right thing."

He looked up at Matrek and scowled. The elf champion almost stepped back. How did the dwarf do that? How could the vaghan intimidate him with little more than a glance? "What is it you're trying to say, vagha?"

"Listen to me, you pompous fishmonger. By now the morehl are close to Balgavarr. If they take the city, all the Kafnysan Mountains are lost. Cyrea will be next. Freedom will be lost. They will return to Tulgesh with an army and kill anything and anyone they find alive. They will hunt down every creature of Nature and eradicate them. Like it or not, you still need the vagha, and we need you. This is our last chance. If the morehl are not stopped here and now, both our kind will be exterminated – or worse."

Despite his feelings, Matrek heard the truth in the young dwarf's words. Although he despised all dwarves at the moment, he knew that, for now, he had to set aside those feelings or his people would suffer for it. "You have a plan, then?" he asked.

Geril almost smiled. "You still have troops that can fight. With your eagles, horses and maybe a coral ship we can arrive at

Balgavarr in a few hours, hopefully before the morehl conquer the city."

Matrek shook his head. "Our place is here. Even with what limited force I have, it should be enough to retake our city."

Geril sighed. "Let whatever morehl are still there have it for now. Come with me to Balgavarr. If we survive, in exchange for your help the vagha will come and help you rebuild what has been lost."

The coral elf's eyes gleamed. vaghan stonecrafters could repair the damage to Tulgesh much faster than the selumari could. What Geril was offering was beyond price. The dwarves were the masters of stonecraft and charged richly for their services.

While Matrek considered the offer, Thrag yawned and sat up. He tensed and unsheathed his claws, but seeing that his friend was unharmed did not attack. Geril grinned at him over his shoulder, glad to see that Thrag was his old self, and apparently free of the poison. Only when Thrag seemed to relax did he turn back to the champion.

"What do you say, Matrek? Do we have a bargain?"

The champion smiled for the first time in what seemed like weeks. He gestured for his troopers to put away their blades. "Tell me your plan," he said.

The screams of the wyverns signaled the beginning of the battle for Balgavarr. The beasts and their riders flew in with the sun behind them, firing their pistols at anything that moved. The crack of their shots echoed throughout the hills. Three foolish vagha that had wandered away from their refuge screamed and fell as hot lead balls ripped through them. They were the first casualties.

The dwarves were surprised for only a moment before they rallied.

Lifting their crossbows, they fired at the winged beasts. The sky was filled with deadly bolts that most of the riders evaded, but several struck home.

Two wyverns shrieked as they were mortally pierced. They plummeted like rocks, their riders screaming in terror until the moment of impact. The dwarves cheered as they ducked back out of sight.

Even as crossbows were reloaded, the goblins broke from the cover of the trees and charged the archers. Crude slings hurled round stones with remarkable precision, but the sturdy vaghan armor and helmets deflected most of the missiles. Disregarding the pain of the sharp stones on their bare feet, the goblins leapt over boulders and through the brush nimbly. The twang of a hundred bowstrings heralded the anguished screams of the trogs as sturdy ironwood bolts pierced pale, grimy flesh. The sure aim of the vaghan marksmen took them down by the score. Wearing only thin skins and no armor, the bolts were as effective as morehl pistol shots at close range. Black blood stained the mountainside.

Still they came. Many got past the archers and threw themselves at the dwarves who were reloading their weapons, leaping over embankments with their stone hatchets flailing, or tearing at the defenders with sharp claws and biting teeth. The dwarves were surprised at the ferocity of the trog attack, but recovered quickly. Only a few were lost to the goblin horde as they turned back the attack. Some managed to bring up their crossbows, and at point-blank range the bolts exploded through the sallow flesh of the swamp-born. Blood sprayed and fell like rain everywhere. Those who could raised their blades of lethal vaghan steel and hacked the enemy with a ferociousness the goblins had not expected.

As the battle turned in favor of the dwarves, the wyverns returned. Now that the archers were distracted, the riders dove from the azure skies and took aim. Firing their guns, lead shot tore into both dwarves and goblins. The sure-footed vagha took fewer casualties by using the slightly taller goblins as unwilling shields.

With hoots and growls, the trogs fell back to the trees to lick their wounds and regroup. The morehl commanders moved among them with clubs and whips, cursing them for cowards and poor fighters. The goblins cowered and swore to kill more dwarves on the next assault.

The vagha quickly counted their own losses. Less than a score of warriors lay wounded or dead, and the mountainside was littered with the corpses of goblins. The dwarves had accounted for themselves well, but unlike their foe, they mourned each loss. An older wizard and his two apprentices moved among them, calling magic to raise the spark of life, healing what wounds they could, returning soldiers back to the fight.

The wounded were carried back into the city on hastily crafted litters through secret tunnels, and those dead beyond raising were laid carefully out of the way for burial later. The bodies were covered with rockblankets that hid them from possible predators, including the goblins, who were known to eat anything.

Axes were wiped clean and crossbows reloaded in preparation for the next time the goblins attacked. Hearing of the losses already sustained, the Elders sent eight units of footmen to reinforce and protect the archers. More heavily armored than their comrades, they were eager to spill trog blood and avenge the deaths of friends.

The respite was brief. Screaming and waving their hatchets, the goblins charged again.

Taran gritted his teeth and swore out loud. At this height and with the wind rushing past, he doubted anyone would hear. Bueron was a coward.

More than a dozen riders still circled the skies above Balgavarr. And what were they doing? Watching and waiting. True, they had taken losses, but to believe that they would not was foolish arrogance. Only two had fallen, and a few others had taken only light wounds from bolts. Unfortunately, Bueron was not among those injured.

The chance to arrange a stray fatal shot had not come up, but Taran was ever watchful for the opportunity. If only they would attack. He could maneuver behind the commander and hopefully… If the dwarves fired enough of their missiles, perhaps Bueron would be hit by one of them, or at least appear to be.

Looking down, he saw that the goblins were launching another offensive. The dwarves had called in ground troops to protect the archers, but they were still outnumbered. They would have to fall back or be wiped out completely.

Bueron was waving a small red flag, the signal to attack. "Finally," he muttered. It wasn't hard to position himself behind the commander. He checked his pistol to make sure it would fire at the crucial moment. Bueron nodded at him and pointed down. "Now is our time for glory!" he shouted.

Taran grinned.

It was his time for glory.

The wyverns dove.

The confidence of the dwarves evaporated as the trogs poured from the trees. The first assault had obviously been a ruse to bolster their hopes that the mountain could be easily defended. Bolts flew in a rain of pain and death, felling goblins by the score, but still they came. The archers managed one more volley before the goblins were upon them. The footmen yelled the ancient battle cry, *"Sa'Balgavarr kava ne!"* – "Sons of Balgavarr to glory."

They waded in with axes swinging. The archers dropped their crossbows and grabbed their own blades as the trogs rolled over them like a wave.

High above, the riders took aim on the dwarves. With the mayhem below, potential targets usually did not stand still waiting to be shot. Taran directed his mount to fly directly behind Bueron. The commander was foolishly unaware of the location of all of his riders. As the riders fired their pistols, Taran had already centered the bore of his flintlock on the back of Bueron's head.

He pulled the trigger.

Among the elder races, the staunch and valiant vagha were well known for their skill in combat. On their home terrain, they could move with speed and grace unparalleled by any other race, and coupled with a fierce desire to protect their lands they were terrors on the battlefield. Yet none of that made a difference when faced with such overwhelming numbers.

The dwarves gave of themselves knowing they faced Death, yet none of them hesitated. Every swing of their weapons dropped goblins even as they were struck down. Blood flowed as the two races traded blows, but the vagha were beaten back until only a paltry few remained. Those cleared a path and retreated into the mountain, sealing the escape tunnels behind them. The trogs cavorted and raised their voices in a loud victory cry despite the heavy losses they had suffered.

"A fine plan," Matrek mused. "You have a good head for strategy, vaghan. You think like a selumari." The champion stood before a table covered with maps and charts. This small house near the harbor was one of only a few that still stood undamaged, and Matrek was tired of the dirty holes he had been sleeping in for weeks. In less than a day the city had been cleared of what few morehl had remained behind. Laman had obviously been unaware that so many selumari had survived, or had not cared. Possibly he thought that after conquering Balgavarr he could return to Tulgesh and recapture it. Geril sat cross-legged against the wall near the door. Thrag waited outside with the remaining elf troops.

He raised an eyebrow. "Does the cunning of my people count for nothing among the coral elves? We are warriors of Nature, the same as you."

Matrek rolled his eyes. "I meant no disrespect. Your idea is a good one." The champion turned to the elves that occupied the small earthen room.

"Geril suggests a ship to take us to Balgavarr. How many can be salvaged?"

The Portmaster of Tulgesh stepped forward and unrolled a scroll. "One vessel, Lord Matrek. The morehl scuttled all but the *Seadancer*. It is a small yacht, but sailable. It requires only minor repairs to be flyable."

"How long?"

"Repairs are almost completed, milord."

"Good!" Geril said. "By now the morehl have reached the foothills near Balgavarr. We need to leave at once!"

Matrek whirled and glared at the young dwarf with narrowed eyes. "I still command my people, Geril. You would do well to remember that. We are still your best hope for a quick return to the Kafnysan region." Turning back to the Portmaster he asked, "How many of our troops will the ship hold safely, and how long will it take to reach Balgavarr?"

"The *Seadancer* can transport one hundred troopers, milord. With such a load, it would usually take two days to reach the vaghan city. Should the winds favor us, perhaps less than a day."

Geril wisely kept his mouth shut. The delays were maddening, but Thrag was still recovering and in no condition for a prolonged flight, especially carrying him. The coral ship was his only option.

Matrek almost smiled at the conflict so clear on the face of the dwarf.

"Saol, step forward," he commanded.

The evoker moved from the hallway and bowed to the champion. "We serve the selumari and Nature, lord Matrek."

"Can the three of you summon the winds? The *Seadancer* needs to travel a great distance in a short time. Magic seems to be the only answer."

Saol gave a quick nod. "This we can do. The winds will blow strong at your command."

"Then let us begin." He turned back to Geril and slapped the table. "We will save Balgavarr and avenge Tulgesh. We sail this day!"

Bueron slumped in his saddle as Taran's shot took off the top of the commander's head. The wyvern, sensing that its rider had been injured, bellowed and dove for the ground. Its actions were too late. Bueron toppled from the saddle and plummeted to the earth. Taran's laugh went unheard. He was now the leader of the riders, and on his way to gaining wealth and power among his people.

"Taran!" a rider called.

Turning, he saw Sheff scowling at him. "You murderous traitor!" his friend shouted, his own pistol up and aimed at Taran's heart. "Bueron knew you would betray him someday!"

Taran heard the shot and felt a hammer blow to his chest. He slipped from his saddle and into the open sky. His last thought was that out of all the morehl, he would have never have thought Sheff loyal to Bueron.

Consciousness was gone before he hit.

Chaos ensued among the riders. Without Bueron, each of the riders sought to wrest leadership from the others. They turned on each other like starving trogs over a bone. Wyvern attacked wyvern with claws and tails, knocking riders from their saddles. The attack on Balgavarr was forgotten as the battle in the sky did more damage than the dwarves could have managed.

In the end, only three of the original twelve wyverns remained, and one was without a rider. Seeing what had happened, the three made a hasty truce and decided to mutually blame the losses on the vagha. They spun their winged mounts gracefully and left the mountain.

The vagha of Balgavarr barely had time to catch their breath before the assault on their mountain began again with another wave of goblin muggers, followed by the wardogs and leopards. Footmen and sentries met the charge, leaping from hidden burrows and dealing death with lethal blades. From caverns higher up, the mammoths charged. The thick pads of their wide feet made the earth tremble as they rushed to the enemy a dozen strong.

The trogs squealed in terror as the huge beasts deftly avoided the vaghan troops and hurtled into the mass of dirty and sallow soldiers. Goaded from behind by their morehl masters, the goblins lifted their hatchets and struck back even as they were trampled. Pelted by hundreds of small, hard missiles and bleeding from deep cuts, the massive steeds crashed down, killing more trogs beneath their bulk. The riders were rent to pieces by the leopards if they survived the fall.

With the slaying of the mammoths, the morehl soldiers at last moved up. The surviving goblins cowered under the ruthless gaze of their red masters, but gripped their hatchets tightly and yelled another hoarse battle cry to show their enthusiasm for slaughter.

The dwarves fell back again, retreating into tunnels and sealed them with triggered avalanches of rock. Unable to find any hidden portals, the morehl horde began the ascent of the mountain.

Wizard Rannon glared down from the stones. Things were not going well. Most of the crossbowmen were dead, and almost all of the mammoths.

A few had been held back in reserve, and would be sent out only as a last resort. The footmen had been decimated as well, and only the goblins had taken the brunt of the counterattack. The morehl were now advancing up the mountain. They were still far distant from the city entrance, but little was left to stop them. He turned to the theurgists and thaumaturgists of the guild. "Our time has come," he said. "Let us see what magic can do for our people."

Arcane power crackled in the air. Joined together, the magic users drew a vast amount of energy from the heart of the world. Rannon gathered the motes of summoned energy and formed them into spells. A sudden wind gusted from the west, bringing with it a cloud of blinding ash. A hindrance to the dwarves as well as the lava elves, but with the vagha safe inside the mountain only the morehl would be affected. More power surged through him. The ground beneath the elves began to shift as the rock changed into a thick churning mass of gooey mud. The heavy troops of the morehl were slowed. Some time had been bought, but not much.

Without hesitation, Rannon called more power. Red and gold motes swam in the air before his eyes. He gathered a handful of the gold and cast them to the sky. The power swirled in a whirlwind of golden radiance. A darkness formed at the center of the vortex. *"Dracon avok Lestros!"* Those behind him gasped as they realized what the wizard was doing.

The magic exploded over the mountaintop. A roar of bestial rage sounded through the portal that Rannon had opened. "Get back inside!" he yelled over the clamor.

"Master, do not do this!" one of the theurgists shouted. "Not Lestros!"

The winged golden serpent shot from the gateway with a shriek of pure rage. Few dared to summon one of the elemental dragons. Only magic could drag them from their unseen abode and back to the realm of Esfah, their first home. The most powerful mage could not hope to control them. Now Rannon quailed at the sight of the massive creature he had called. The sweeping wings cut the mountain air with a hiss, and the gaping mouth flashed wickedly sharp fangs, each longer than a grown dwarf's arm. Now Lestros the Dread flew over Balgavarr. Cries of panic wafted up from far below, and the wyverns of the morehl cried in terror as the riders guided them down.

The dragon eyed the small figures of the dwarves standing on the summit, then at the army of morehl spread down the mountainside. Craving the destruction of the puny things, the dragon banked toward the lava elves.

Suddenly it turned and dove towards Rannon and the theurgists. The wizard gaped and then turned to flee. The opening down to the city was only a few steps away. A blast of air knocked them from their feet as Lestros passed overhead. The long sinuous tail snapped down and smashed into the rocks with a crash that echoed through the mountain. The boulders covering the entry were reduced to rubble from the strike. Most of the magic users had made it inside, but two theurgists remained, and they looked at him with eyes wide with fear.

Rannon choked on dust and got to his knees. He had no choice now but to face the dragon. He stood, his staff supporting him. Lestros wheeled around gracefully in the sky, seemingly turning on one wingtip. With a screech like thunder, it dove towards the wizard again. Frantically they called for more magic and cast it out as brilliant sparkles of light that surrounded the tapered head of the dragon. This might buy them a few seconds to find a place to hide.

Lestros flew through the cloud of dancing lights without pause.

Opening its mouth, it exhaled a stream of noxious breath that blasted into Rannon and the theurgists with the force of a hurricane. The theurgists wailed in terror. The wizard's skin tingled and he felt fear as he realized what was happening, and that he was powerless to stop it. The breath transformed him and the others into stone.

Passing over the peak, Lestros turned its attention to the vast army below. Eagerness glinted in the faceted eyes of the earth-drake. It was time to feed. With another roar of anticipation, it dove.

"This was my grandfather's axe," Geril said, stroking the shaft of the weapon. The crescent blade shone in the bright sunlight. Far below the ground was a blur as the ship flew. The winds summoned by the evokers were propelling it at dizzying speed.

"Really?" Matrek eyed the blade. "I possess my father's sword. He used it in his youth when the trogs of Deepmire attacked Tulgesh. That battle lasted many days, but no goblin survived. It passed to me when he died."

Geril nodded. "My grandfather's name was Zephras. Fresh from battle training, he was sent to one of our remote Tower outposts on the western slopes of the Kafnysans. Trogs attacked there shortly after he arrived. They crept in on a moonless night, killing the sentries and taking the tower by surprise. Only my grandfather and a few others survived, but they held the tower until reinforcements arrived. He lost the axe during the battle and was forced to start clubbing goblins with his gauntlets. That is how he came to be called, Thunderfist. Many years later he saved our city from a dragon with this same axe."

"A dragon? With naught but an axe? Tell me this story, vaghan. It seems you have a minstrel's talent for tall tales."

A grim smile crossed the dwarf's face. "I did not see what happened, but my father Ghuren was there, and he would not tell his son a story that was not true. They never knew where the death-drake came from. Dragons must be summoned to the land from wherever their realm lies, yet this one came upon Balgavarr without warning.

"Most of our people were inside, but an unlucky few were caught outdoors when it appeared. Our warriors were quick to attack the beast, but our bolts and axes were ineffective against the thick hide. When the dragon was enraged by the attack it reared up. Zephras rushed under the drake and sliced its belly open, killing it."

"A true hero he was. I hope he was honored as such."

"The dragon fell on him as it died. My grandfather was killed. When they recovered his axe, they gave it to my father, who has since passed it to me. I carry it to honor both of them."

Matrek clapped Geril on the shoulder. Despite the dwarf having thwarted his possession of the Magestorm relics, he respected bravery, and this particular vaghan came from a long line of courageous fighters. "You will honor them this day, I think. There will be much morehl blood to spill; may your blade drink deep of it."

Geril stared at his reflection on the blade. "It will drink," he said. "By the rage of Eldurim, I will quench its thirst."

The selumari coral ship raced through the skies.

Laman cursed the foolishness of the vagha while admiring their tactics.

Retreat to safety and then summon a dragon. Brilliant. The beast had passed over the mountain and was now diving on his army. "All missile troops," he called, "ready your weapons and fire at my command!"

There was no time to try and counter the dragon's attack by summoning another, and the necromancers would be unable to send it away since they could not work the earth-magic that had summoned it.

Lestros banked its wings and glided over the army. The spade on the tail arced down and into the troops. All dove for cover, but many that did not move fast enough were either smashed into pulp or cleaved in two. The dragon crashed down with stunning force. The impact caused the earth to heave and hundreds of morehl soldiers were knocked off their feet. Lestros lunged and attacked. Each swipe of the long tail hammered into the soldiers, and only a few avoided the strikes. The razor-like claws sliced troops by the dozen. The triangular head snapped down again and again, swallowing soldiers in great gulps. Blood flew every time the jaws closed.

A squadron of bladesmen led by a duelist crept in as Lestros paused to roar. Striking with their swords, they inflicted minor wounds but effectively drew the attention of the dragon. Lestros reared and prepared to strike.

This was what he had been waiting for. "Fire!" Laman yelled.

The thunder of a hundred pistols rolled and Lestros shrieked as the lead balls struck it. Blood spurted from countless wounds and rained down, the hot blood burning many of his troops before it could be wiped away.

The dragon faltered as death claimed it. The wings folded and the jeweled eyes dulled as the life drained from the drake. The golden hue of Lestros's scales faded to the dull gray of granite as it crashed into the hillside, scattering millions of coarse pebbles and jagged scree across the terrain, centered around the creature's corpse like an inverse crater.

Laman sighed and shook his head.

The attack of the drake had proved costly. More than forty of his troops lay wounded or dead. The rest of his troops, however, seemed energized by the drake's defeat. They appeared to gain strength before his very eyes, rising back up and screaming battle cries.

"Enough of this," he growled. The dwarves were becoming an annoyance. He turned to his subordinate battle leaders. "Begin the march. We assault the city now. All troops attack."

A morehl saluted and raised to his mouth a horn made from a dragon's tooth. The loud call was eerie and sounded unnatural. Even inside the mountain city it echoed and raised the hackles of the vagha. There was no mistaking the intent behind the malevolent wail. The lookouts posted on the mountain sent messengers scurrying with the dire news that the morehl were attacking. In a red and black armored mass, they raised their voices in a triumphant war cry and rushed the mountain.

"Prepare for siege," Vors shouted. "We don't have much time." Word had been brought back that all families had been evacuated safely to the northern forest of Dur'sona. The warriors waited tensely. Axes and crossbows were readied, and armor checked and rechecked. The warriors knew that they were outnumbered almost three to one. They would face the minions of Lord Death this day, and die as valiantly as they could, taking as many lava elves with them as possible. Balgavarr would not be an easy victory.

Warlord Kile waited with troops of footmen and patrollers at the main doors. His two hundred soldiers waited for the gates to open. Axes were held tightly as they set themselves to meet the charge of the morehl. The gates would not open until the elves were in sight, and then just long enough to let them out before closing again. They were going to their doom, but so long as one warrior of the vagha remained, the fight would not be finished.

The gates creaked open, and the vaghan defenders rushed out, voices raised in their own furious battle cry. The morehl were just cresting the last slope.

With an avalanche-like crash, the two armies came together.

"Faster!" Geril shouted. From his vantage point at the bow of the flying coral ship, he could see that the main force of the vaghan army had been deployed and were engaging the morehl at the city gates. If they were defeated there, the city would be lost.

They had only been in the air a few hours. As they left Tulgesh in the early hours before dawn, the evokers had summoned a powerful wind that filled the sails and pushed the ship almost faster than the eagle riders could keep pace with. Now, as the sun peaked at midday, his home was in view, and what he saw filled him with despair. The morehl were seemingly endless.

How could they hope to defeat such an army?

The ship began to descend.

Thrag sauntered up next to him and pointed over the rail. "Fight," he said. "Fight now."

"Your big friend has the right idea," Matrek said from behind them. "I agree with him. The time is now."

Behind the selumari champion, the troopers waited with weapons ready for battle. Despite the eagerness in the eyes of the soldiers, Geril knew they would not be enough. It was hopeless. He turned to tell Matrek that he should return to Tulgesh and salvage what he could. He and Thrag would do what they could here. Matrek's eyes went wide and he rushed to the rail, pointing towards the mountains. "What in the name of the gods of Nature is that?"

Geril looked and shouted joyously. Thrag roared and the selumari cheered.

A mass of figures was coming over the top of the mountain and making their way down the mountainside to the gates. Darker shapes knifed through the skies above them.

The feral and frostwings had arrived.

## PART 9

*The price of freedom is often high and great sacrifices must be made to ensure peace. A single life is nothing. To face Death for a just cause is not martyrdom, but the greatest gift one can give his people.*

*—Zephras Thunderfist, vaghan hero*

With a sword that dripped blood and gore, Laman fought. The vorpal blade sang as each opponent was felled. No shield or armor could withstand the magical weapon, and he had lost count of the number of dwarves that had been sent to Lord Death at his hands. He remained unscathed, with hardly a scratch on his own armor. The battle was going well for the morehl.

Although the vagha fought fiercely, the superior numbers of the lava elves would soon overwhelm them. Balgavarr Reaches was theirs. Nothing could stop that.

The horn sounded again and he looked up, momentarily distracted. The horn should not sound unless the enemy rallied. His dwarf opponent took the opportunity to use his axe and parry what should have been a deathblow. His return strike clubbed into Laman's side like a hammer, and only his plated mail kept him from being sliced in half. Still, it felt like he'd been punched by a dragon. He snarled and knocked away the dwarf as he stumbled from the battlefield.

Once clear of the fighting, he scanned the mountainside for what had caused the horn to sound again. What he saw he could not believe. From the summit of Balgavarr mountain swarmed a huge gathering of beastly shapes that walked upright and held weapons like a humanoid. He shook his head as if to clear away what had to be a delusion. The ghwereste were dead, killed off during the battle at Seshara years ago! Now had they returned in time to aid the dwarves? How? What were those things flying above them? Dark-winged creatures that even now began to hurl spears of crystal ice with deadly accuracy were swooping over the mass of his army. Morehl soldiers fell with cries of alarm and pain as they were pierced by the crystal spears. This was not possible; it could not be happening!

The surefooted feral moved quickly, covering the distance between themselves and the morehl with swift strides that brought them into the thick of the fray mere moments after their arrival. With screeches, roars and growls, they engaged the elves with unparalleled fury, allowing the dwarves to fall back to rest and regroup.

The other creatures dropped from the sky and went to work with axes of sharp stone. A group of massive white bears charged into the midst of the black-armored elves and wreaked havoc, tossing his soldiers like so many insects. Not expecting such allies to appear, the morehl troops were caught off-guard. Still, they recovered and fought back with the ferocity they had been trained to use in battle.

Laman could not believe the carnage as it unfolded around him. His soldiers were being slaughtered, despite greatly outnumbering the dwarves and feral… and whatever these other creatures were. But with his army surprised, the result proved devastating. Shoving the vorpal sword into its scabbard, Laman turned and rushed back into the treeline where the necromancer, Duroc, and his group of magic users waited. The sight of a selumari coral ship flying toward the mountain stopped him. *Now what?* Where had the coral elves come from? He sprinted into the trees.

The necromancer waited with his group of warlocks and adepts in a small clearing. Nearby, the vaghan wizard Latkis sat trussed and gagged. The sight of the dwarf gave Laman pause, but only for a moment. He'd thought the wizard dead in Tulgesh. Grabbing the dark mage by the robe, he shouted into the face of the startled elf. "Summon the undead. Call them now, before all is lost."

The feral poured over the mountain in unimaginable numbers that astonished the vagha even as they cheered. The frostwings continued to plunge from the heights and send their icy spears down in a hail of death.

Geril could not help but smile as he saw what effect the surprise attack was having upon the morehl. It looked likely that the day would not be lost. The lava elves had not been expecting such resistance. "They made it!" Geril shouted.

"This is your doing?" Matrek asked.

"It is." Grinning like a child presented with a new toy, he watched the feral leap into battle.

The flight from Tulgesh had been incredibly swift, yet he had chafed at every lost hour. Thrag had slept most of the way and now seemed fully recovered from his ordeal with the swamp stalker poison. Even the bare patch of skin on his side had regained a small growth of black hair, and the self-inflicted cuts had healed to pale scars. The devastator stood next to him at the rail and watched the battle. He could almost sense the eagerness that showed on Thrag's hairy face. Sharp fangs were bared in a rigid grin of expectation, and the red eyes shone brightly.

The *Seadancer* was still some distance from fields below the mountain, but he was no longer as concerned. Matrek assisted the captain of the vessel in choosing a landing site close enough to join the battle, but far enough from the battle to keep the ship from becoming a target. The troopers lined up by the rails and readying their weapons. They talked softly among themselves and Geril was surprised at the viciousness of what they planned. Each trooper had lost friends and family at Tulgesh and looked forward to avenging each loss.

A dark shadow on the ground in the distance caught his eye. From the west it grew and spread as it approached his home. His eyes narrowed as he tried to see inside the shadow, but they were too far away. "Matrek?" The champion left the captain to join Geril.

"What is it?" he asked the dwarf.

Pointing to the darkness that continued to approach Balgavarr, the dwarf asked, "What is that?"

Matrek stared for a moment, then sighed. "Nature preserve us," he said. His hands held the rail so tightly his arms trembled.

"What is it?" Geril asked again, fear growing inside him.

"Just what we didn't need. The undead."

"Milord?" One of the sailors called from the stern. "I think you should see this."

"Now what?" Matrek growled. "As if things aren't bad enough."

Joining the young elf at the rail, Matrek, Geril and Thrag stared southeast at a strange red cloud. "I thought it was a trick of the light, milord," he said, "but it does not change, and it is coming closer."

The champion peered with narrow eyes. "That's not a cloud. Those are some kind of flying creatures. Many of them."

Geril stared but could not see what Matrek was talking about. The eyes of the vagha were sharper in the dim and dark of underground tunnels. "Can you see what they are?" he asked.

"Like nothing I have ever seen before. They carry weapons that look to be on fire, and what look like crossbows, but smaller than your people's weapons. I don't like the looks of this."

"They could be coming to help us, milord," the sailor offered.

Matrek frowned. "Not likely. An old war adage of my people says: Always expect the worst, and you will never be surprised." He looked back over his shoulder at the captain standing by the wheel. "Get us on the ground now." There was no mistaking the seriousness of the order.

Thrag growled at the red cloud following them. "Scalders," he spoke with a soft whispered growl.

"Scalders?" Geril asked. "Is that what they are? How do you know of them?"

Thrag blinked. "Faeli. Steamdancers." His husky voice was thick but clear.

Geril gaped. When had the devastator become articulate? "Thrag? Do you know these things?"

The shaggy head nodded once as he spoke slowly. "From the deepest regions of the Plaguelands they come. Seeking battle and bloodshed, they do not care which side they fight for. Only once have they come to the Shadowlands, and never again." The words were guttural and Thrag seemed to cough them instead of speaking, but Geril had no trouble understanding.

Still, why had Thrag waited so long to show that he could speak the common tongue?

"Your people fought them?"

Another slow nod. "For two risings of the sun we battled, and many of the frostwings fell from the scorching touch of the faeli. In the end, we drove them from Icehome."

"Why are they here?"

Thrag turned his concerned gaze to his smaller friend. "They will see who prevails and fight them." With graceful lopes, the devastator made his way to the bow of the ship. Raising his head, he let loose a mighty howl unlike any Geril had ever heard. He and the selumari covered their ears, amazed that any living creature could produce such a noise. So close to the mountains, the cry echoed across the hills.

In the air and on the battlefield below, the frostwings heard the cry of their leader. Those already in flight banked and flew toward the *Seadancer*.

The rest erupted from the ground, leaving the still bodies of morehl and trogs behind. Like the wave of a tsunami, they rode the currents of the wind and circled the graceful ship. Thrag vaulted from the vessel and joined them, his wings strong once more. With cries and barks he welcomed his people, then showed them the approaching scalder horde. Watching with wide eyes, Geril saw the hatred and animosity of old losses bloom on the faces of the areosa. Hundreds of long crystal spears sparkled into view and axes were waved menacingly as the frostwings flew to meet the scalders.

Geril swallowed hard. "Take care, my friend," he said, hoping and praying he would see Thrag again. The sails were furled as the ship came to the earth, and the landing poles were extended to keep it from rolling over.

Rope ladders were thrown over and the selumari swarmed over the sides, swords already drawn and expressions of pure bloodlust and rage on every elven face. Not being as long-limbed as his companions, Geril had more of a struggle leaving the ship, but managed to reach the rocky ground after waving off several offers of assistance. Matrek soon joined him as the troopers lined up.

"You vagha continue to surprise me," he said.

"Oh?"

"Finding the feral and enlisting their aid. Even I believed them lost. I never would have thought it possible." He slid his cutlass from the scabbard and admired the shining blade. "Now it is time for me to avenge the losses of my people. Let's go save your home."

High over Balgavarr, the frostwings and the scalders came together like separate storms, and the resulting clash sounded like thunder. The deep throaty roars of the areosa and the shrill screams of the faeli as each engaged their old and bitter enemy were a cacophony that rang in the ears of all that heard. Flaming maces spewed sparks as they clashed against the hard iron of the frostwing axes. Small sharp bolts were fired from the handheld crossbows the scalders carried. Frostwing warriors cried out and fell as they were struck, even as lethal spears of ice were flung to impale the lithe red-skinned bodies.

Screams of rage and pain intermingled in a deafening chorus as the wounded and dead began to fall from the sky.

The stench of rotting flesh signaled the arrival of the undead. Like a black fog they slowly moved from the trees, and the bright daylight seemed to turn gray and cold as they advanced. Creaking skeletons of every race led the march waving scythes and old rusted swords long buried beneath the soil of Esfah. Behind them came ghouls and wights carrying clubs and sharp daggers of bone. The moaning and wailing of the dead soldiers filled the vagha with crippling fear. While staunch defenders of Nature, the sight of the hideous troops was more than most could stand, and they fell back even further.

The ghwereste were surprised for only a moment. Perhaps of all Nature's warriors they feared the abomination of the undead less than the rest. Their creation had been Nature's response to Lord Death's nuisance of the undead, and being made of the valiant beasts of Esfah, they felt no fear of things long dead. While the hatred the feral felt for the morehl was great, it did not compare to the loathing that filled them and drove them to destroy the lifeless beings. Lead hunter Eihwaz brandished wicked fangs and roared his rage at the sight of them. Sheathed claws extended as he grasped the cord-wrapped handle of his thick stone blade. "For Nature!" he roared. Leopards and lynxes rallied to his shout, as did the stalwart cavalry of buffalo, horses, and antelope. Bounding down the slope of the mountain, they charged into the mass of animated corpses and deathspawn.

The wails of the dead increased as the feral ripped into them with claw and blade. Body parts and chunks of fetid flesh flew. Zombies and revenants struck back and inflicted their own hits on the attacking feral, leaving broken and bloodied figures in their wake. The animal-folk did not yield. They continued to fight as the fallen soldiers of Death rose back up even after they were hacked apart.

At the rear of the legion, a lich guided the movement of the soldiers of decay. The empty sockets of the skull were lit by an unnatural red glow. It walked slowly as it hurled death magic to raise the fighters felled by the ghwereste. The moldering robes whispered like the souls of the damned as it swept black motes of magic from the air and cast it onto the fallen warriors.

The magic stirred the remains, caused scattered arms and legs to reform into whole bodies that slowly stood erect again. If the lich had been capable of laughter, it would have been cackling. A battlefield held no lack of death magic.

Eihwaz cut through a mob of skeletons, shattering the dry and brittle bones with every blow, his goal a tall armored figure swinging a greatsword with deadly accuracy. Instinct told him that this was the leader of the undead troops. If it were to fall, the Legion would lose guidance and the ghwereste would triumph. His stone dagger shattered another skeleton into dust, and the knight turned to face him. Raising a massive kukri broadsword, the Legion commander brandished it fiercely. The tiger never hesitated and charged the knight. Blocking a vicious thrust from the sword, he plunged his stone blade through the rusted armor and into the chest of the knight. The reeking figure fell back staggering but did not fall.

The tiger warrior pursued relentlessly, striking repeatedly at the tall figure of the undead knight. Hissing savagely, he hammered at the corpse, driving it further from the troops it commanded. The knight managed to block most of the hits, but many struck true, opening bloodless wounds in the pallid flesh. The sword flailed ineffectively against the attack as the knight shielded itself from the worst of the strikes with the blade. Eihwaz refused to let up. Instinct warned against it. Stories told how the dead felt no pain, and how they never grew tired. If he yielded even a moment the knight would strike back. Only by removing the head would the knight be truly dead and beyond reanimation.

Eihwaz overextended a swipe with his claws and the knight used the opening to slice a ghastly wound in the tiger's side. The hunter fell back with a grunt, dropping his dagger. Guarding the vicious wound, he crouched. The knight advanced to finish the kill. Raising the broadsword over its head, it brought the blade slashing down.

The tiger dodged the blow and leaped. Razor-sharp claws dug into withered tissue as he sunk his long fangs into the throat. Gagging on the taste of putrid flesh, he barely felt the sword as it plunged through him. Blow after blow pounded the long dead knight as the claws began to rend off strips of emaciated hide. With a wrench, the tiger tore the head from the body and hurled it away. The two bodies crashed down with the hunter on top.

Eihwaz rolled off the corpse and glared at the sword that impaled him.

Dark spots swam in his vision and the hunter knew the wound was mortal.

With a primal scream, he pulled the blade from his middle and fell back. If Caulte found him in time, he could be healed.

Until then, he would save his strength. Closing his eyes, he dropped into darkness.

Because the knight leading the undead forces was thrown down, the undead troops lost their cohesion. The assault quickly fell into chaos as the undead soldiers began to wander about the battlefield, no longer acting together as fighting units. The feral were quick to pull them down and destroy them. The glare in the eye sockets of the lich grew brighter as fury grew within it. How had the knight been dispatched so soon in the battle? No amount of magic would reanimate the fighter again. Without the knight to lead them, the Legion lost the ability to function. The lich retreated into the cover of the trees. It could sense the power of the morehl necromancer nearby. Turning from the battle, the lich moved toward where the necromancer and his adepts waited.

Geril saw the hunter fall. "Gods, no," he whispered. He looked up at Matrek. "We have to help him."

"There is a great deal of fighting between us. He is perhaps better off for now. The undead will think him dead and leave him alone. You should join your people now. My people will engage the morehl. The feral have them occupied, so you should be able to sneak past and into the city. Go now."

Geril did not hesitate. Holding his axe, he ran through the trees toward home. If luck smiled on him, he would find Caulte and see that he knew about Eihwaz.

Most of the remaining trogs and morehl he encountered failed to notice one lone dwarf scampering by. Those that tried to stop him either backed away when he waved his axe, or were cut down. Goblin, lava elf, or undead, nothing could deter him. He wanted to go home.

Laman wrinkled his nose as the smell of rot drifted on the breeze. The lich said nothing as it drifted by. Duroc stepped back as the stench wafted over him. "What do you want?" he asked.

"Only magic can save this day for your people," came the voice, a rasp like broken glass. It gestured to the feral leaping and slashing among the undead and morehl troops. "Look upon your them and see your doom." It turned to Laman. The red eyes flared. "Imbecile," it snarled, pointing a skeletal finger at the conqueror. "Had we known the ghwereste would come to the aid of the vagha, the Legion would have been better prepared. How could you let this happen?"

Overcome with anger, Laman strode up to the lich and placing both hands on the bony chest shoved it away. It fell with a rattle of bones in a bag.

The vorpal sword was in his hands in the blink of an eye and at the throat of the dead mage. "How could I let this happen? I have no foresight. I thought them dead long ago, dead at the hands of your legion. This is not my fault. What do you intend to do?"

The lich seemed to float back upright. "We must combine our magic… Our death magic. I have the knowledge we need to finish off the feral and the dwarves forever."

Duroc looked nervous. Combining magic was tricky and dangerous.

"What can we do with magic besides raise the soldiers we have lost?"

"Morguus Ebraxus."

The two words stunned the necromancer and his adepts. Laman watched their reaction with amusement and a little trepidation. "Would someone like to tell me what that is?"

"He wishes to summon a wyrm," Duroc gasped.

"A dragon?" Laman shouted. "Another one? We already had to deal with one lizard and you want to summon another?"

Duroc glared at the undead mage. "Not just any wyrm, milord. Morguus Ebraxus is one of the worst of the death wyrms, and he has a particular hate for the dwarves of Balgavarr. While it is true that the beast could very well finish the dwarves and those damned animals, I have no doubt it would turn upon us as well. To summon it would be madness."

Laman turned away and surveyed the carnage of battle taking place on the mountain. The lava elves were losing ground rapidly and were in retreat.

The vagha and feral were in pursuit. The trog forces were all but gone.

Above the peak the scalders and frostwings remained locked in combat, and it appeared that the steamdancers were not faring well. Slender red bodies were falling like rain. "What else remains for us to do?" He turned back to the others. "Call the wyrm. Let it destroy the dwarves. We'll still win the mountain once they have sated the dragon's hunger. As for me," he said as he drew his sword, "I will see the inside of Balgavarr this day, or not at all." He ran toward the city.

Taking Duroc by the arm, the lich pulled the protesting necromancer to the edge of the trees. "Call the power of Lord Death," it rasped. "I will cast the summoning spell. Morguus will not resist our call."

Black motes of unholy energy surrounded the mages. Duroc gaped.

"There is enough magic here to summon more than just the wyrm," he cried, as the force of the magic vibrated in the air.

The lich slowly raised bony arms high as dark magic swirled around it.

"*Dracon avok Morguus Ebraxus!*"

Geril found a group of four vagha footmen fighting a troop of ten morehl near the main doors of the city and charged to their aid. Swinging his battle-axe, he waded into the fight. Coming from behind the lava elves, he struck down three before they were aware of him. His sudden and surprising appearance caught the morehl off-guard and allowed the dwarves to overcome the remaining bladesmen before they could recover from the surprise of an attack from the rear. Then he was greeted warmly by the warriors. They clasped his hand and pounded him on the back, welcoming him home.

The youngest, a youth he remembered as Hergat, thanked him for his help. "We saw the frostwings, Geril. How did you find the feral? Where did they come from?"

"The luck of Eldurim," he replied. "I'll tell the tale later, but for now we must win this war." He motioned over his shoulder where the morehl were in retreat. "They must not get their reserves into the battle. Any reinforcements now could be deadly for our people."

Hergat looked confused. "We thought this was the last of them," he said.

Geril shook his head. "You have just seen a part of the whole. Even now the rest of them are marching toward the city. Even with the feral and frostwings, it may not be enough to turn the tide of this battle." He quickly chose three of them to be messengers. "Get back inside and tell them to send out everyone they can spare. The morehl must not breach the city seals. Tell my father I have returned." They looked stricken, and in the aftermath of their silence, Geril knew that Ghuren was no more.

"How?" he said, speaking past the lump in his throat.

"No one knows, Geril," Hergat said softly. "He was found far from the gates on the southern slopes. We think a morehl patrol found him, but there were only two sets of footprints. Rannon said that he had been dead too long to awaken the spark of life. I'm sorry."

*How could Ghuren be gone?* "I'll grieve later. Now do as I say." In contrast to his unfeeling words, his heart was a dull thud in his chest.

They ran off as a rumbling of the earth shook the group. "Is that an earthquake?" asked Egan.

Another rumble, and Geril cursed. "There is nothing natural about these quakes. Something is wrong."

An ungodly screech reverberated over the mountain as another shudder racked the peak. The morehl had reached the trees and were concealing themselves among the thick trunks. The ghwereste paused in their pursuit and looked around with anxious expressions on their furry faces. Almost as one they wheeled and began to flee the battlefield. Geril knew then that something was dreadfully amiss. The feral could sense danger and obviously knew something was terribly, terribly wrong. The tremors were just a sign of something far worse.

Another shriek of bestial fury, and his eyes found a distortion in the air down the slope. A black shadow hung in the air and was writhing as if alive and in pain. He felt it then, the prickling of his skin that warned him that magic was being worked. The silhouette of darkness stretched and warped, becoming larger. To the dwarf it looked like the eye of Lord Death himself.

He thought he knew what would come through that sinister portal, and his worst fears were realized as a black snout appeared, quickly followed by a spade-shaped head. Eyes as black as bottomless pits glared as it pulled the rest of its scaly body through the opening. The thick-plated black hide rattled as it shook itself free from the hole, the long tail cracking whip-like in the still air. Lengthy talons dug into the soil as if the wyrm sought to injure Nature herself. Raising its head on the long neck, it screamed primal rage to the heavens. "Firiel and Eldurim protect us," Geril breathed. "The fools have summoned Death himself, and he comes in the form of a dragon."

Morguus turned and the ebony eyes took in the single small figure.

Geril swallowed and gripped his axe handle tightly. He knew it was foolish to remain where he was, but something held him in place, unable to tear his eyes from the black depths of the wyrm's eyes. The jaws parted, showing wickedly pointed fangs. With a growl that made the air quake, it started toward him. The massive body crushed trees and the slain bodies of dead goblins, lava elves, and dwarves.

Footsteps scrambled behind him as another secret portal opened in the hillside, and nearly fifty dwarves emerged into the daylight at his back.

Carrying crossbows and battleaxes, they spread out and faced the wyrm. He blinked as he recognized an older warrior. "Elder Vors?"

The Council member wore dented mail and carried an old and scarred battleaxe in one aged hand. Geril recognized the weapon. The thick spike above the curved blade was Vors' own addition years earlier. It made the axe distinctive, and it had hung in the Hall of Honor for decades. The blade shook slightly, as did the voice of the old dwarf. "I will fight with you this day, sa'Ghuren. I owe that to your father. I will fall, but I will die a defender of my home."

Geril watched the wyrm crawling up the side of the mountain. "And when you fall, who will lead our people?"

Vors turned to the younger dwarf and gently laid his hand on Geril's shoulder. For the first time in his life, Geril could see kindness in the old eyes of his family's oldest antagonist. "You will," he said.

High over the forests of Dur'sona north of Balgavarr, the areosa and faeli remained locked in a titanic struggle. Small bolts and ice-spears filled the air until the scalders ran out of ammunition for their diminutive crossbows. Realizing they would be at the mercy of their old enemy, they moved in closer and engaged them with fiery maces. Even with the greater size of the frostwings, the scalders fought with reckless abandon.

Their lithe scarlet forms seemed to phase in and out of existence, making them nearly impossible to hit, though their weapons administered little damage on their glacial adversaries. Many of the frostwing troops did suffer burns from the scorching touch of the scalder defense, but few of them fell.

Among the scalders, Lirk wielded his mace and screamed his anger at every missed strike. Every frostwing that dodged out of the way only increased his fury. The faeli had come with only a small force, expecting most of the battle to be already over with. Instead, they found the dwarves still holding the mountain and their old enemies, the areosa, aiding in the defense.

Now, the scalders were being killed on every side, and less than fifty out of three hundred remained.

One of the larger beasts flew too close, and Lirk lashed out with the mace. It veered away and blocked the strike with the heavy, round shield it carried. The return hit from its axe struck before Lirk could evade. The blade sliced into his right shoulder, severing the right arm and wing cleanly. Lirk fell screaming to the rocks far below.

After the successful kill, Thrag wheeled and dodged other attempts to kill him, panting with excitement as his claws shredded wings and opened lethal wounds in the slender forms. At his barked command, the areosan magi summoned a bolt of lightning that struck in the midst of a large group of the scalders, shattering bodies and filling the air with red blood. The faeli inferno mage desperately tried to summon magic, but found that the motes seemed to disappear as they were called. Too late it realized that the areosan mages could absorb the magic it summoned, and while distracted, the devastator king had flown up from behind. Thrag struck with the force of a thunderclap. Battered and broken, the remains fell to crash into the trees far below.

With the killing of the inferno mage, the heart went out of the scalders. Thin wings flapped frantically as they veered almost as one and flew shrieking away from the victorious frostwings, leaving Balgavarr far behind.

The areosa pursued a short distance before being summoned back by Thrag's roar. The devastator pointed to where the black wyrm was rapidly closing the distance to Balgavarr. The battle was not over yet.

Caulte slowly picked his way across the ravaged slope of the mountain.

The aged wolverine leaned heavily on the golden staff he carried. The uneven slope and fallen bodies made slow going for his old bones, but necessity demanded he try. Eihwaz lay injured a short distance away, and he was determined to save the life of the hunter. All around echoed the raucous noise of the battle with the dragon. The entire mountainside trembled with it.

Reaching the wounded tiger, he knelt carefully by his side. He winced at the wound and placed one trembling hand over the gash. A sigh of relief escaped him. The hunter still lived, but the life-force was fading. Perhaps he had come in time.

Laying the staff down, he shakily got to his feet and steadied himself.

As powerful as the dragonstaff was, the power it could summon was of no use now. He spread his arms and summoned the power of the air.

The dwarves howled their defiance of the wyrm's threat and rushed the beast. Charging down the slopes, they raised their voices in a cry echoed throughout the range. Geril led the charge, swinging his axe and screaming until his throat was raw. From behind, the archers fired their crossbows. The bolts bounced ineffectively off the thick armor but took the dragon's eyes from the small figures rushing towards it. Sharp axe blades hacked into the scaly hide but did little damage.

The great head reared back and the dragon shrieked in anger. Then it swept down and into the crowd of vagha surrounding it. The long horns that swept back over the skull from the brow flung the warriors aside like insects.

The tail cracked like a whip and scattered even more. Small bodies fell lifeless to the earth or were crushed under the bulk of the twisting serpent.

Still, they came. The dwarven footmen poured from the mountain, each one of them willing to give his life in defense of his home. Every warrior that could be spared issued forth from the city, screaming war cries at the dragon.

Geril ducked a swipe from the claws and swung his axe with all the strength he could muster. Normally the thick scales of the dragon's hide would have deflected an edged weapon, but the keen edge shattered through a thin patch of scales on the foreleg and bit deep into the flesh beneath. Thick black blood gushed and Geril dove to the side to avoid the poisonous flow.

Morguus shrieked in pain and jerked back the wounded limb. Geril rolled away as the wyrm attempted to grab him. He swung again and missed, uttering a curse that would have shamed his father.

Mighty jaws snapped and just missed a group of footmen. The dragon lunged and bit, but no feet were surer on a highland slope than those of the vagha, and they leaped to safety. Geril cheered them but knew that despite their affinity for the mountain, many would die if something was not done soon. He was about to call for a retreat when a blast of cold air swept over him and a barrage of ice-spears came raining down upon the dragon. Geril whooped as the areosa flew overhead. More spears showered down and struck true. Morguus shrieked again as it was stuck. Geril almost felt sorry for the beast; for he had seen the frostwing spears thrown into solid rock.

Distracted by the flying creatures and in pain, the wyrm reared up, exposing the soft belly. Old tales told to him by his father surged from his memory. Thus had his grandfather died beneath the crushing bulk of the dragon he had slain with his last blow. A small price to pay for the lives of his people. He rushed in.

Morguus crashed back down before he had taken a dozen steps. The eyes of the wyrm followed the flight of the frostwings, and the baleful eyes blinked slowly. With growing alarm, Geril heard the slow intake of air. That could only mean the dragon was about to spew its disease-ridden breath at the ice warriors. If that happened more of his friends would die. "Rally!" he cried. "Do not let it use its breath!" He charged.

A lone warrior wielding an ancient crescent blade beat him and the others to the serpent. As the dragon lifted its head, Vors rammed the long spike on his axe between the scales on the neck just as Morguus exhaled a black stream of filth into the sky. The breath cut off abruptly, but not before Geril saw five blue shapes fall from the sky.

Thick black blood spewed from the wound and covered Vors. The elder screamed in agony as his flesh began to rot. Chunks of flesh began to fall from his slumping frame and he moaned. He fixed his eyes on Geril. "You must lead," he said, his voice barely a whisper that the younger dwarf heard clearly in spite of the noise around them. Then he fell over, dead, his skeleton already beginning to dissolve.

The dragon was wounded but far from dead, but the many wounds were taking their toll and it was weakening. It shook its long neck back and forth to try to free the axe that still hung there. Gripping his axe, Geril again ran to the dragon. If Eldurim's luck shone on him, he could cause it even more pain.

The spade-shaped head swiveled and the emptiness of the black eyes seemed to impale him. His steps faltered and he almost fell. Fixed in the murderous hypnotic gaze, his axe slowly dropped to his side. Panting, Morguus raised one massive foreleg. Talons like razors and as long as his arm unsheathed and swiped down to disembowel the small figure.

If the blow had landed, Geril would have been eviscerated where he stood. Instead, he was knocked aside by a heavy body covered with thick fur and was sent flying. The painful impact brought him back to his senses. With a moan, he struggled to his feet. What had hit him? He had been about to strike when everything went hazy, and then... The dragon roared. Geril looked up and saw Thrag dodging blow after blow of the mighty claws, while throwing a constant stream of ice missiles at the wyrm. Leaping almost a full dragon's length into the air, the devastator swooped in close and sent a long icicle directly into one black eye. The serpent shrieked in pain and lashed out suddenly. The talons struck true. Dark blood misted the air as

Thrag was knocked from the sky. When the heavy body hit the earth, the realization struck home, and Geril cried out as he saw the crumpled form of his friend lying still on the ground. The dragon was nudging the body with its snout.

Despair clutched his heart and squeezed. The agony of seeing his friend lying so still was the worst pain he had ever felt. Rage filled him. Pure and unchecked, it spread through his body. The tiredness in his limbs was erased and new strength coursed through muscles that bulged. Gripping his axe, he screamed his anguish.

Geril chose his path.

His muscles filled with unimaginable strength. With a single, mighty bound he leaped, the jump carrying him over thirty paces and onto the neck of the wyrm. Startled from his attack, the dragon's head smacked into the ground. Geril straddled the neck and gripped hard with his knees. The dragon reared, trying to unseat him. He raised the axe over his head and brought it down with all his might. The half-moon blade sank deep into the skull. With a loud crack and a shower of sparks, the weapon cleaved through thick bone and into the brain. The damage was done. Morguus Ebraxus let out a shuddering groan as the sinuous body slumped to the earth and grew still.

The dragon lay dead.

Yanking the axe from the skull, Geril slid from the neck and stumbled to where Thrag lay. The devastator lay unmoving on his side in a growing pool of blood, his wings crumpled under him. "Oh no," Geril breathed as he knelt by his side. Dropping the axe, he grasped Thrag's shoulder and carefully rolled him over onto his back, gasping when he saw the four deep cuts crossing Thrag's abdomen. He shut his eyes at the sight. How could Thrag survive such a mortal wound?

The devastator drew a ragged breath and opened his eyes. The light in them was pale, but he focused on the dwarf. "Geril?"

Geril smiled and patted Thrag's hand. "Easy, my friend. I'm here to help you." Closing his eyes, he concentrated and sought the power of fire.

With magic, he would fan the spark of life and heal his companion. Thrag would live. Thrag had to survive. Opening his eyes, he lifted his hands to grasp the motes.

The air was empty.

Desperately he tried again, and once more the magic failed to respond to his call. "No," he hissed. With a sudden realization, he knew why the magic would not come. He had taken the path of the warrior to slay the dragon, and once chosen, he could not turn aside from that choice. The magic he had once been able to sense so easily was now denied him.

"Geril."

He looked into Thrag's eyes. "I'm sorry. It won't come. What can I do?"

Thrag lifted his hand and grasped the dwarf's arm. "Dying," he rasped, a slow trickle of blood seeping from the corner of his mouth.

Geril placed his hand over Thrag's. "Hold on, dear friend. It will be alright. I'll get help." Tears were making tracks through the grime on his cheeks.

The devastator's breathing was ragged. "One… life… for… all," he said, his voice growing weak.

"No, Thrag," Geril said, his voice catching in his throat. A thick lump was growing there, making it hard to talk. "Don't leave us. We need you."

"One… life," he said again. He was panting now, as if the exertion from speaking was draining the last of his strength. His hand squeezed Geril's arm almost painfully. "Geril… friend?"

"Always, Thrag. Our people will always be friends, and we will sing of your bravery in our songs for all time. Rest now and save your strength."

Thrag's arm fell to his side. He took a deep breath and spoke a name. "Ra'al," he said as the light slowly faded from his eyes. The thick chest did not rise again.

Geril shook him. "Who's Ra'al, Thrag?"

He did not respond.

"Who is Ra'al?"

But silence descended upon the mountain, and the vaghan warrior broke it, raising his voice in a howl of grief.

# PART 10

*"The strongest evidence of love is sacrifice."*
*—Del sa'Brinn, vaghan bard*


Geril hung his head. How could this have happened?

"How touching," spoke a voice behind him. "A valiant creature. Still, it might make a nice rug."

Geril lifted his head and looked over his shoulder as his hand grasped the handle of his axe.

One of the morehl stood behind him. By the armor and the helm, the vagha knew he was looking at one of the lava elves' generals. The red elf held a humming vorpal sword in one hand.

"You speak far too lightly of a creature with more honor than any of your kind will ever know," Geril spat.

The elf uttered a dry laugh. "Honor? A foolish concept cherished by foolish people." His eyes scanned the mountainside and the devastation that had scarred the natural beauty. "I suppose I have you to blame for whatever these creatures are. I will admit they stymied my use of the scalders. Did you bring the ghwereste as well?" Seeing the dwarf glare at him was answer enough. "That may have cost me this war, and I cannot accept that. I never expected what I saw here today, but it will avail you nothing. Your city is mine, and so is your life!" The vorpal sword screamed as Laman swept it up and brought it whistling down.

Geril dove over Thrag's body, rolled onto his knees and swung his axe.

The two blades met with a jarring *clang* just over his head. The impact knocked the stunned dwarf back and he almost let go of the axe. Dropping the weapon would mean his death. Laman held the sword out before him as he advanced. A wry grin was on his face and his eyes narrowed. "Warrior of Nature, can you not accept that my race is destined to rule Esfah? Now you die."

Geril scrambled to his feet and lifted his axe. Never before had he felt so confident and powerful. Fear should have drained the strength from his limbs and made him cower before the more experienced warrior that faced him, yet he braced his legs firmly and glared at the elf. "Come kill me then," he snarled, "and let me introduce you to your Lord." The axe weighed nothing as he held it.

Laman lunged and Geril blocked the thrust with an upswing of his own blade, and again the impact of the blades echoed across the mountainside.

The conqueror tried to hide his surprise. This dwarf was strong, far stronger than any dwarf he had ever encountered before. The fact that there was no fear in the eyes of the vaghan disturbed him. The small warrior waited for his next move. For the first time he could remember, Laman felt uncertain. *Enough!* It was time to remove this pest from his sight and plunder the city and its riches. He swung the sword to decapitate the runt.

Geril saw the blow coming and blocked it again, the two blades ringing. The vibration traveled painfully up his arms, but he held true. Again the morehl swung his blade and was countered. The sword left bright arcs across his vision as he struggled for his life. Each blow from the sword chipped another small piece from his axe. Slowly he was forced back. The elf seemed tireless, and Geril's arms were beginning to grow heavy. The elf kicked out with his leg unexpectedly, catching Geril in the stomach and driving the breath from his lungs. He stumbled and fell but managed to keep his hold on the haft.

The elf loomed over him with a triumphant grin. "Only one race will rule Esfah, dwarf, and it won't be yours. Die knowing that your people will serve me as my slaves. I, Laman, will rule Balgavarr." He lifted the sword and thrust it at Geril's heart.

This war and the destruction that had been wrought upon his home, coupled with the death of Thrag, caused Geril's blood to boil. Rage and hatred seethed in his soul, pushing him to the brink of madness. When the lava elf attacked, he met it with a fierce calm. Focusing his emotions into his counter-strike, he jumped to his feet and swung the weapon of his grandfather, Zephras Thunderfist, with all of his might.

In the back of his mind he heard a rumbling, as if the gods were casting bones to determine his fate.

The two blades met in a concussion of conflicting powers. With an explosion of magical energy, the vorpal sword shattered. Geril felt the haft of his axe split in his hands.

Laman was flung backwards several paces as his cherished sword was destroyed. The backlash from the release of energy blinded his eyes and seared his hands as it threw him to the ground by the blast. Laman recovered rapidly, though his ears were still ringing. He tried to pull his belt knife and get to his feet, but a solid blow to the side of his head knocked him back down. Sprawled on the ground, he was unable to grasp how he had ended up in this position. Cold metal touched the side of his neck. "On your knees," said the husky voice of the dwarf.

The edge of the axe never left Laman's throat as he slowly got up.

With the handle splintered and tenuous, Geril held the axe by the head.

Laman's eyes were having difficulty focusing, but he could make out the outline of his opponent like a shadow in fog. A trickle of dark blood ran down the dwarf's neck and into his armor.

"Call off your attack on Balgavarr and you will live."

He refrained from laughing. Laman asked, "Do you think my army will stop just because I tell them to? They want Balgavarr as much as I do. They would kill me if I ordered a retreat."

"Then why should I spare your life?"

The elf looked up. His vision began clearing and he could see that the dwarf was not speaking in jest. If presented with a good reason, he might spare the life of an enemy. *A weak failing of Nature's chosen ones.* He met the eyes of the dwarf. "You can't," he said.

Geril nodded. He took the blade away from the neck of the elf and lifted it to strike.

Laman jerked the knife from his belt and lunged. The dagger struck Geril in the thigh, plunging deep into his flesh and striking bone. The vaghan warrior bellowed as Laman laughed. Now he would grab his backup short sword and carve the dwarf's heart from his chest.

Before he could move Laman saw the flash of polished metal in the sunlight. Geril brought the axe down with all of his strength behind it. The blade sliced through Laman's helm and cleaved the skull beneath. Blood sprayed and splashed the earth. Not until it sliced into the heart did the blade stop. The body trembled for a moment before growing still. Geril pulled the axe free from the corpse and watched unfeeling as it toppled over. "Welcome to the Reaches," he said, then spat on it. Not even Lord Death could resurrect the body that had once been Laman.

Gritting his teeth, he wrenched the knife from his leg, and tearing a strip from his shirt, he bound the wound. A horn sounded and he looked up. The remainder of the morehl army charged from the trees and into the clearing where the body of the slain dragon lay in the sunlight. They waved their weapons and fired their pistols as they shouted their war cry. Geril's heart sank as thousands of the red-skinned soldiers poured from the trees.

Even with the added warriors of the feral, frostwings, and coral elves, the armies of Nature were outnumbered.

Despite a valiant defense, Balgavarr would be lost. The selumari met the initial charge and for a moment brought the morehl to a standstill with the fierceness of their attack. Led by Matrek, they found themselves quickly surrounded and attacked from all sides. Still, the valiant elves left more of the enemy lying broken and bloody on the ground than they lost. However, unless the rest of Balgavarr's defenders went to the aid of the selumari, they would be destroyed. He gripped the broken haft of his axe and prepared to take out as many of the black-armored warriors as he could before he was cut down.

Soft footsteps behind him. Looking back, he saw the gray-whiskered face of Caulte. The aged shaman leaned heavily on his dragonstaff and seemed to be on the verge of collapse. "Tired, these old bones are young Geril. Healing our hunter took the last of my strength."

Geril fought the urge to yell. "What are your people waiting for? The morehl will wipe out the coral elves, then move to the city. What are they doing?" He waved his arm angrily at the feral army gathered far away from the melee that was taking place below them on the slopes. They had spread out in a line and were preventing the vagha from rushing to the battle. The dwarves held their weapons and stood in confusion, wondering if the feral had turned against them.

"Fear not," Caulte said with assurance. "All will be well. They keep back your people for their own protection."

"Protection from what?" Geril growled.

Caulte lifted his staff pointed to the skies. "From what the areosa prepare to do. To the elemental make-up of your race it could be deadly."

"What do you mean? I don't understand." He turned to run down the hill and fight, but Caulte's hand took hold of his arm with surprising strength.

"Do not be a fool," he said. "Watch and see the power of the frostwings unleashed."

A crackling filled the air and drew Geril's eyes upward to where the magi of the areosa and his group of magic users flew in a graceful circle. He knew that they were summoning magic, but could no longer sense the power being called. His eyes could see the crystals that were swirling in the air at the center of the formation and growing into an enormous ball of ice that threw off fingers of bright lightning.

As he watched, the frostwings flew behind their creation and formed a wedge in the sky. They opened their mouths and roared, and the magic they had summoned took a new shape and flew from the heights. The titanic cone of frigid air blasted against the mountain. The temperature dropped so suddenly Geril's breath seemed to freeze in his throat. Snowflakes danced as they dusted the entire area. His skin began to tingle and he backed away as he felt the menace in the spell.

On the battlefield, the magic had a more dire effect. The selumari felt the air grow cold and looked around with wonder on their faces. Among the morehl, the spell caused much more havoc. As Geril watched many of the soldiers simply fell over, frozen in mid-strike. Ice covered the bodies and clawed at those lava elves still standing. Their movements grew sluggish and the swords in their hands dropped slowly. Seeing an advantage and apparently protected by the presence of Ailuril within them from the glacial cold of the magic, the selumari began to slaughter the nearly helpless morehl. The scorpion knights found their hideous steeds immobilized and easy pickings for the cutlasses of the blue elves.

As the cold began to seep away and the snowflakes melted, the feral and the vagha charged into the thick mass of incapacitated morehl. The feral ran with screeches and cries of bloodlust. They had regrouped after decimating the undead troops with few losses of their own, before holding back the vagha. Geril recognized Eihwaz among them, growling orders to his people. Many cast the crude but effective spears they carried with deadly accuracy, impaling the morehl but leaving the selumari soldiers unscathed.

The coral elves sounded the horn again as they shot their longbows. The frostwings dropped from the sky, ice spears crystallizing and flying into the mass of the morehl horde. Geril saw scores of duelists, bladesmen, scouts and spies fall as they were impaled where they stood. The barrage of missiles was deadly. The armies of Nature took only minor wounds from a few lucky pistol shots, fired from quivering hands unable to draw a bead.

The morehl had only crossed a third of the clearing, and more than half their number was dead or seriously wounded. Lacking a leader to guide them and still suffering from the areosan magic, their weapons dropped to the earth. Surrounded on all sides by hundreds of warriors of various races, they saw the futility of fighting any more and surrendered.

Geril sighed as his axe sank to his side. The battle was over.

The last morehl stragglers had been captured. Their weapons had been gathered from the field of battle and cast into large and growing piles. The vaghan smithies were already at work melting them down to be reworked into tools and other non-lethal items. None would be remade into weapons.

Geril and Caulte sat near the main doors to the city and watched the activity. Geril's mouth was dry from talking for almost the entire afternoon.

As the daylight waned, he began to think about finding a tall mug of ale and his own bed. He was too tired to even mourn his father, though grief for the old warrior and Thrag threatened to overwhelm him.

Caulte had listened without comment to the story of his adventure in Tulgesh, but had applauded Geril's solution to the problem of the Magestorm relics. News of the stalkers in Deepmire had raised the hackles of the elderly shaman, as did the report of the poison they used to reproduce their numbers.

"This may cause trouble for the selumari if these stalkers decide to leave the swamps," Caulte said. "Have you warned Matrek?"

Geril nodded and wiped sweat from his brow. He was now craving a bath to go along with the ale. "He dismissed it as a delusion from spending so much time in the swamps. The fool hears no voice but his own at times. When the stalkers attack Tulgesh he'll sing a different song and claim I never warned him." He plucked a blade of sugargrass and poked it between his teeth. "What happens now, shaman? Can you see the future?"

The wolverine rasped what passed for a chuckle. "There is no need to foresee what is easily discernible. The ghwereste will return to Seshara. After many years, the longing for our home has become a fever. Some of our number will escort the remaining morehl beyond the plains back to Saugor's empire on Mount Uruzak. Let their ruler decide the penalty of their failure."

"What of the frostwings? What happens now that Thrag is gone?" He choked as he spoke the devastator's name. That pain was too fresh.

"Most will return to Icehome. Some will travel to Seshara as guests of the ghwereste, and others will remain here for a short time if your people will allow it. The areosa do not fear the gaze of Death as they did before. They will do as we all must do. They will go on."

"Did you know that Thrag was always able to speak the common tongue?"

The wolverine looked away and chuckled. "I did. The areosa do not like the speech used by the lowland races. It hurts them to use it, so they speak very little. Even my people find this language difficult at times, but for the frostwings it is even more difficult. Forgive him the small deception."

Geril chewed the blade of grass thoughtfully, mulling over the last words that Thrag had spoken. "Caulte, who is Ra'al?"

The wolverine turned and stared at the dwarf. "Where did you learn that name?"

"Thrag spoke it, just before he died. Who is it?"

Caulte sighed. "Ra'al is Thrag's offspring. Still just a kitten and born just before he left Icehome to hunt in the lowlands where the two of you met. The selumari would call him a prince regent. In time he will grow to be their king."

Geril nodded. "I thought as much. I was worried that… What is it?"

The shaman had stiffened and was sniffing the air. "Magic is being summoned. I feel it."

Geril shrugged. "Of course you do. All of the race's mages are using magic to heal the warriors."

Caulte shook his head, his whiskers trembling. "None of them are capable of calling death magic save the areosa, and this magic does not feel like theirs. Someone is calling a large amount of black magic, and I fear what they may do with it. I will find Eihwaz. Meet us at the edge of the clearing."

Geril got to his feet as Caulte limped off quickly. "Eldurim's beard, now what?" Lifting his axe from his belt, he trotted down the hillside.

Duroc and the lich combined their power as they sought the power of death magic. The foul stench of the undead mage made the necromancer want to vomit, but he swallowed the bile and concentrated on the magic he helped conjure for the enemy. Duroc wondered what use the lich intended them for. "I do not like this," he said. "Our army is defeated, why are we still here?" His adepts nodded agreement. He wanted to flee, but some overpowering need to exact vengeance kept him near the vaghan city.

The blazing sockets turned to him. "We will summon Morguus once again, and another dragon, and another, until they destroy this mountain."

"Morguus is dead! They killed the deadliest wyrm known, and you want to bring another? This is madness!"

"Fool," the lich hissed. "A dragon never truly dies. If killed, it can be called again." His sneer was less effective with lips shrunk in a rictus grin. "The true master of the bloodless horde in the Shadowlands wants his enemies hobbled."

Duroc stiffened his lips. He knew only rumors of the mysterious undead commander in the north, but had assurances that Saugor had met with him in years past. "Call it quickly, then. I do not wish to be captured and delivered to my Emperor in chains."

The lich would have sniffed in disdain if it had had a need to breathe. Instead, it walked a few steps away and swept a bony arm through the air, conjuring the power of their corporate magic, drawing it to himself. The power it held was almost too much for it to control. It thrust its arm into the sky. Streamers of black magic shone from between the clenched bones of its hand. "*Dracon avok Morguus Ebraxus!*" it cried, throwing the magic down into the clearing.

The power exploded and a black vortex formed. Cries of alarm sounded as the coral elf horn blew again. The lich threw back its head and cackled.

"Come and claim them, great Lord! They are yours!"

A ghwereste tiger and wolverine suddenly burst into the trees where the magic users stood. Behind them followed a single dwarf, half a step behind with his legs pumping furiously. The feral roared their rage as they spied the lich.

The necromancer and his adepts backed away from the fury of the enemy. "Your time of victory is over," shrieked the lich as Eihwaz charged. There was no time to summon more magic to evade the attack, and the lich had lost its scythe in the battle. With a single graceful bound the hunter leaped, crushing the lich beneath his heavy bulk. A roar of pure hatred split the air as Eihwaz used knife and claw to shred the wretched being into dust.

Drawing short poniards, the adepts threw themselves at the dwarf and wolverine. Geril evaded a poorly thrust blade and cut one of the adepts down with a single deadly stroke across the midsection, spilling bloody entrails onto the ground as the adept screamed. Another darted in and was clubbed unconscious.

Caulte lifted his arm and summoned his own magic. Casting a streak of magical energy into the clear evening sky, he called a bolt of hot white lightning that crisped the necromancer where he stood. For a moment, the ash held the shape of an elf and then collapsed. The two remaining adepts cried out, terrified, and fled into the trees.

A bound dwarven form sitting against a tree caught Geril's eye and he rushed to the side of his wizard friend. Using his belt knife, he cut away the bonds that held the magic-user and pulled the gag from his mouth. Latkis grinned at him. "Your timing is almost flawless, sa'Ghuren. I am glad to see you, but we must do something to help our people fight the dragon."

Dark shapes hurtled toward the vortex. The spiraling pool of dark magic was about to birth the monstrosity that was Morguus. Geril cheered as the areosan mages flew around the vortex. "Worry not, Latkis," he cried as he helped the elderly wizard to his feet. "Our winged friends may solve the problem for us!"

Black streams of power looked as if something was siphoning it off from the pool. Geril traced them to the source: it appeared that the frostwings were absorbing it—dispeling its power. The swirling vortex of dark magic flickered and went out like a candle in the breeze. The cry of the wyrm was heard once through the breach, a shriek of fury and vengeance denied. Then it faded away.

Balgavarr remained free.

## EPILOGUE

The mists poured out from crags of the mountains far above. Far below, the Heimdarl Crag opened into a canyon of winding passageways that had frosted and thawed for generations.

Deep within, an undead king sat upon his frozen throne. With sunken skin stretched paper-thin across the bone, Leisterbane watched as his roving bands of undead minions entered his hoary chamber.

As the skeletal hunters approached wordlessly, only the scraping sound of the bodies they dragged made any noise at all. The minions knew what the masters commanded, especially their leader, the knight who still wore the selumari armor of the long-gone kingdom of Lurneville on the far side of the globe that was Esfah.

Leisterbane glanced aside at one of his generals and nodded to him. Only few of those under his charge had been granted autonomous free will. Leisterbane knew freedom to be dangerous… but he was not so foolish to think he needed no peers to clarify his thoughts and refine Leisterbane's plans.

The general was once a vagha and his eyes had long since decayed and the skin of his face torn free. Ony a frosted beard remained. The dwarf bent to check the bodies.

One body was covered in crystalline dirt, only recently exhumed. The other was a shriveled and shrunken thing with a body that drooped limp and no legs.

"Some kind of reptile," the dwarf wheezed. "Flesh for the hordes?"

Leisterbane stood. The baleful glow in his eyes blazed bright. "It is no animal," his voice boomed. "This is one of the sarslayan."

He walked towards the corpse with the puckered scales and caressed its face; Leisterbane peeled back the eyelids and stared into the milky, white orbs as he drank in the creature's essence. "This one was a powerful spell caster and an acolyte of Death. He will serve Father Malgrimm perfectly."

The dwarf cocked his head, but said nothing. Gray whiskers from his white beard wagged and several of them shed, floating down to the floor like autmn leaves in the dustlight.

"We must replenish what forces we lost and we need a new general to lead those with an eldritch bent."

The faceless general dragged the corpses behind the throne and set about his work. Bubbling in the deep crack where the planetary crust split wide, an inky pool of wild necralluvium roiled like an angry mass of insects. The dwarf scooped up a handful of the goo.

Leisterbane took his seat again on the throne. The lich in his service had been an impulsive fiend with a strong will. It did not bother Leisterbane to have lost him… especially considering what he gained in the bargain.

A cancerous, toothy grin crept across his Leisterbane's pale face. Long ago, he told the young morehl King Saugor about the Magestorm weapons and the red elf had been fixated on them ever since.

To get them, he knew Saugor would eventually fling his full might after Balgavarr and so he'd engineered the frostwings to be caught in the crossfire. Their king had to die.

Leisterbane could not have played his hand any more perfectly. He cared little for the weapons of war. While others of Esfah's myriad races fixated on those creations churned out by the gremmlobahnd, Leisterbane's purposes were far loftier.

The undead did not need to destroy the races. They need not enter any needless wars. He could send out rovers for centuries and the frostwings could continue to pick them off and destroy them whenever they left the cover of the Shadowlands' thick mists… eventually, they would find what Leisterbane sought... and then he would kill a god... *the god*. Leisterbane would kill Mother Ghaeial and all life on Esfah would cease.

The undead's plans all along had been to eliminate Thrag. Long had the areosan leader harried the tundras and sent fliers to keep the undead in check. With the frostwing gone, a vacuum in leadership would undoubtedly change things.

As the dwarf touched the two new units' faces with his goo-slicked hands, the necralluvium took hold. It stretched across the bodies like hungry worms and the bodies drank in the fluid with a wicked, osmotic process before binding to the spinal cords where the magic of the fluid took hold, animating the corpses.

The first shambled on uneasy legs. The second undulated upon its segmented form and presented itself to Leisterbane; a stark, malevolent intelligence burned within the creature's eyes.

Leisterbane could wait for what came next. He was good at waiting—he'd done it for a thousand years—and finally, his time would come... only a little while longer.

He watched the undead troop walk further down the halls of the Heimdarl Crag and take its position there amongst the others. Motionless skeletons and other undead soldiers stretched as far as could be seen. *Only a little while longer. With no areosan king, Leisterbane could finally send out his hordes to roam unchecked. He would soon put his true plans into motion.*

In the great hall of Balgavarr, a battered and broken axe was hung upon the Wall of Honor for all to see. There among the weapons that had been wielded by the hands of legends, the axe told of the battle to save the city from the armies of Lord Death, and of the dwarf that had used it. An engraved plate of solid gold was hung below the axe. The inscription read: *Wielded by the hand of Geril sa'Ghuren, Dragonsbane, of Balgavarr.* Geril stared at the half-moon blade with a grim smile on his weary face.

The weapon that had been wielded by the hand of Zephras Thunderfist in defense of the city years ago had again saved Balgavarr. Few weapons possessed such a legacy. The solid haft was split down the length, the blade was pitted from Laman's strikes with the vorpal sword, and permanently stained in places by the vile blood of the dragon. He had insisted that it be hung as it was, instead of repaired.

The ceremony honoring his rise to the position of warlord had finished only hours before, and the last celebrants had departed. With the deaths of Ghuren, Rannon, and Vors he had been given a place on the Council and become a leader of the vaghan community. He could take no joy in the great honor, clouded as it was by the death of his father. This, despite the fact that usually a vagha had to pass his first century to even be considered for the Council, and he had not yet reached half that age. The elder dwarf would have been very proud of his son. He turned from the Wall of Honor and left the great hall, his steps carrying him out of the city and briskly up the side of the mountain.

Spring was full upon the mountain. As he moved above the treeline toward the summit, the gentle breeze blew coolly through his hair and beard.

Birds darted among the few scattered bristlecone trees, singing gaily. Tufted squirrels chased each other through the branches. Nature ruled the mountain.

He sighed and continued his hike.

Matrek had not stayed for the ceremonies and feast, returning instead to Tulgesh. His parting words had been clipped and with only a trace of civility.

The selumari champion had honored the new warlord with only the slightest of bows and bade him remember the promise of stonecrafters to help rebuild his city. An entire guild had departed immediately, more than a hundred crafters and their apprentices. Geril had sensed that although Matrek was pleased to find the dwarf keeping his word, there was still animosity emanating from the coral elf. Geril had thwarted him, something the champion was not used to people doing. The relics were gone forever, and Geril would never be able to explain acceptably to Matrek how dangerous he thought they truly were. Matrek was a warrior and only saw that a weapon he might have used had been taken away. Now that this most recent war had ended, Matrek had had time to reflect upon Geril's deeds. The thin ice of peace between selumari and vagha had been cracked. How long would it hold before breaking?

Most of the frostwings had returned to Icehome, but many had remained behind to enjoy the hospitality of the dwarves and to explore the region. Geril had vowed that this alliance would not falter. He commanded that all areosa were welcome anytime, to stay within the city for as long as they wished. The vagha had embraced their new friends wholeheartedly, and it was becoming a mark of distinction to have a frostwing or two staying in one's home.

The path was steeper now as he approached the summit. The vegetation was sparse and the air thin and hard to breathe, but he did not stop to rest until he reached the summit. Then he allowed himself a pause to catch his breath and take in the magnificent view the mountaintop afforded. Far below the foothills and stretching to the horizon lay Seshara. He could see the feral army as a small dark blob moving across the expanse.

The ghwereste had stayed for the first day of celebration before heeding the instinctive call to return to the golden plains of Seshara. Eihwaz and Caulte had pledged peace for their people, and the vagha had gained another valuable ally.

Ambassadors had already been chosen from the many volunteers and were eagerly accompanying the feral home.

At this height the air had a bite to it, but the sun was at midday and warm. The archaic standing stones had no shadows at this time of day, and he welcomed that fact as he walked among them to the cairn of rocks at the center of the ring. The mound was large, and the cracks between the stones filled with mortar so that the seams would resist the weather and potential grave robbers for centuries.

At that moment he would have given his soul to turn back time and change the path he had chosen to follow. As a wizard, he could have summoned the spark of life and saved Thrag instead of watching his friend die. Now the areosan king lay at rest in the most honored place the dwarves could think of. From here he would watch over the city he and his kind had saved from darkness. Born of Death's vile machinations, Thrag had become a valiant warrior of Nature, and a symbol of unity to both vagha and areosa.

Artisans were already at work carving a likeness of the frostwing that would reside in the great hall.

In a way, the areosan was not truly dead, as Thrag would live on in the memories of those for whom he had died to keep free from tyranny.

He laid his hand on the stone mound. "Thank you, my friend. Thank you for my life. I promise that Ra'al will be safe. I owe you that much."

He lifted his eyes from the cairn to the majestic view from the mountain. He took a deep breath of pure crisp air. A sudden love of life and joy swept through him. Something his father used to tell him suddenly came to his mind. *I would rather fail in a cause that will someday triumph than triumph in a cause that will someday fail.* He only now understood the meaning behind the words. For a time, there would be peace in this small part of

Esfah. Elsewhere in the world, the battles between the forces of Death and Nature would rage on. Eventually only one would triumph and come to rule.

With luck, his days of adventuring and battle were over. That was unlikely, but for now, he would be content to live.

## THE END

214

# APPENDICES

# GLOSSARY OF TERMS

Abyss – the home of the Void, a realm where silence reigns aside from pockets of terror and chaos where unknown gods reign. This is a similar concept to Greek myths of an underworld.

Ailuril – the secondborn of the Esfahan gods. She is represented by the color blue and has power over the air elements.

Aguarehl – the fourthborn of the Esfahan gods. He is represented by the color green and has power over the water elements.

Amazon – the race of mankind said to have been deposited whole upon Esfah as one of the few races created by Tarvenehl himself. Amazons are the warrior caste of human race.

Areosa – commonly known as the frostwings, a frigid, felinoid, winged race with magic resistance.

Bloodless – another common name for the undead.

Deadzone – synonym for the Abyss, except from the point of view of the trogs or morehl. Within their respective religions, versions of the afterlife differ wildly and as often as they align in geopolitical goals, neither could imagine spending an eternal afterlife in the company of the other.

Death – the half-brother god who is the child of Nature and Void.

Dragons – these beasts come in two forms: Drake and Wyrm. Drakes have wings, and wyrms do not. Though the dragonkin are a kind of subspecies, they are not the same thing, no matter how similar they are. They used to live hidden across Esfah, but were nearly eradicated in the Dragoncrusades. Dragons have eternal spirits and when they die, they return to to the plane where they now dwell. Dragonmagic came in two forms and it summons them from this realm or from nearby (the older form of this magic which has now been forgotten since these mythic beasts have largely gone out from Esfah.)

Drakufreet – the dragonkin who come from the same realm as dragons and appear as a type of draconic hybrid race.

Eldarim – a human-like race that emerged over eons from Esfah's primordial soup and predated the gods-made races. The eldarim are versatile and have proven the capacity to breed with many of Esfah's races. They are called eldarim, menaing "from the earth."

Eldurim – the firstborn of the Esfahan gods. He is represented by the color gold and has power over the earth elements.

Efflorah – the race of treefolk.

Esfah – the world and one of two planets revolving around Soll.

Empyrea – known commonly as the firewalkers, a war-loving mercenary race.

Faeli – commonly known as scalders or steam dancers. These creatures are fickle and capricious and were once captured and tormented by Death.

Festration – a kind of location so tainted by evil activity that the very land itself has become corrupt and avails itself to wickedness.

Firiel – the thirdborn of the Esfahan gods. She is represented by the color red and has power over the fire elements.

First Age – everything from the beginning of creation to the year 863.

Frehlasuhl – also called the Forsaken or Mudbloods. They are the offspring of selumari and morehl unions. They cannot breed with each other to have children, only with one or the other race, but they are rejected wholesale by both.

Ghaeial – the mother goddess known more commonly as Nature.

Ghwereste – called the "feral folk." These are a hybrid of animal and man created at the dawn of the Second Age.

Kreethaln – there are three of these mystical artifacts made of an unknown metal. Little is known about them except that they each possess some kind of arcane power. Their names are Life-bringer, Wisdom-giver, and Spell-crafter.

Leguin – a sister planet to Esfah that also orbits Soll; it can often be seen in the night sky, appearing above the horizon like a bright star.

Lich – a powerful undead spellcaster. Lichs often possess necromantic capabilities, though their created undead are maintained by force of will, rather than by other means, such as the Necralluvium.

Morehl – commonly called lava elves. They have red skin in addition to their elf-like features and their blood is said to smoke when exposed to air.

Necralluvium – a kind of magical potion with a seeming life of its own. This black filth can kill the living. The dead that are exposed to it become animated.

ditto – the name of the moon. It circulates Esfah twice in a daily cycle.

Sarslayan – commonly known as swamp stalkers. These snake-men emerged in the Second Age as a result of Death using magic to twist the creations of his half-brother Aguarehl. They create more of their kind through magic conversion rather than by reproduction.

Second Age – everything after year 863 of the First Age. This began when Ghaeial walked the face of Esfah and surveyed the damages of the myriad of wars. The 864th year is year 1 of the Second Age.

Selurehl – the name of the second god to emerge after Tarvenehl, usually known as Void.

Selumari – commonly called coral elves. They have blue skin in addition to their elf-like features.

Shara – what the eldarim people refer to themselves as when they communicate with each other. It means "little god-in-the-making."

Soll – the sun.

Tarvanehl – the creator god who came first, according to all mythology and story; he is often known as Father Time, or simply The Father.

Teldrim – a race of extinct horselords that bore many similarities to the amazons. A creation of Tarvenehl, these were remarkable because the race could intermix with any other. They were eradicated by Melkior shortly after their emergence.

Trog – a synonym for goblin. Trogs much prefer to live in boggy areas and tend to pollute the land.

Vagha – commonly known as dwarves.

Void – sometimes used interchangeably with the Abyss or, the power or person of Selurehl who is frequently referred to as Void, just as his son Malgrimm is more widely regarded as Death. Context determines the meaning.

Warchief – a title of rank among the vagha. Below the king is a Warchief who leads Warlords and Warcommanders under them. It might commonly be understood as a sort of general.

# TIMELINE

Included is the general time line of major world events in Esfah. Please note that, during the time before the Mother, Ghaeial, became a goddess and the First Age began, prehistory spanned a scope of time measuring eons, and in that time, verily, only *Time* existed. Despite the sage's attempts to capture much data and ancient knowledge, they did not begin tracking time and dates until the first passing of the Daybringer. The first three years of history might very well have been hundreds or even a thousand years as the gods (and the earliest race of eldarim) kept time differently.

## *Prehistory N.D.*

Tarvanehl exists and creates within the realm of Void/Abyss and Esfah and Leguin are born; Ghaeial realizes she is a goddess and falls in love with Tarvanehl.

Turambar courts Leguin.

Selurehl, third of the brother gods grows angry.

Eldurim the firstborn (earth) god-son of Ghaeial and Tarvanehl is born.

Ailuril the secondborn (wind) god-daughter of Ghaeial and Tarvanehl is born.

Firiel thirdborn (fire) god-daughter of Ghaeial and Tarvanehl is born

Aguarehl fourthborn god-son (water) of Ghaeial and Tarvanehl is born

Malgrimm cursed bastard son (Death) conceived and birthed after Selurehl's violence upon Ghaeial

Eldarim are birthed by Esfah and slowly emerge from the mire of her lands and water, evolving over long periods of time. They call themselves the Shara in their own tongue.


*The First Age*

03FA: the Daybringer Comet passes Esfah for the First Time, the Sisters of Fate are birthed of Turambar and Leguin, dragons and the drakufreet are created during the schism of the god-children.

04FA: Earliest creations of the gods: "monsters" are formed

15FA: Selumari are created

16FA: Vagha are created, trogs are created

17FA: Morehl are created

19FA: The Dawn of War. Morehl invaders overthrow the first selumari

22FA: Humans arrive on Esfah via Tarvanehl's intervention

28FA: Davian Whisperwynd leaves Maris-ta-Sehlim

32FA: The proto-empyreans are birthed in the whirlwind

42FA: Gundraokh Shatterfist finds the Bands of Turambar and renames the city of Orelod to Gundakhor

96FA: Sshkkryyahr the Dread rises to power

103FA: Malgrimm attempts to create a new powerful, destructive force within the Shadowlands, but the areosans' magic resistance helps them maintain mild independence from the Death god and he abandons them to the frost plains.

143FA: Undead created, Melkior is defeated upon the Raithlan Plains by the gods' chosen Champions

167FA: Dilution of the eldarim race and the reduction of the Dragon population via the Dragoncrusades that eliminated nearly all the natural dragons of Esfah; the spells that compelled natural dragons that still remained in the realm became forgotten after this date in favor of those drawing eternal dragons through the interplanar rifts

341FA: Existence of the empyreans is discovered when they aid the elder races in the first major undead uprising.

447FA: *Book of the Land, 1st Ed.* is published and immediately begins revisions

520FA: Morehl city of Karakto falls to the selumari

532FA: Morehl discover cursed bullets and retake Karakto

544FA: Large load of eldrymetallum discovered on the Karakto slopes

562FA: Final version of *The Book of the Land* completed after 23 quintennial installments

836FA: The Magestorm Wars erupt with the tectonic catacylsm that opens the Netherwold and nearly splits Dereh'Liandor in two; the Arcana Veil stiffens

842FA: Disappearance of the gremmlobahnd and the genocide of the drakufreet

863FA: Final battle of the Magestorm Wars ends the first age, the faeli are birthed in the Firequags and captured by the forces of Death, and subjected to torments in the pits of the World Wound

*The Second Age*

01SA: Ghaeial walks the earth and surveys the damage of the elder races.

03SA: Ghaeial creates the ghwereste

79SA: The plagues of the World Wound at its evils continue and the first of the sarslayan emerge from the nearby Snekdenn Bayou

153SA: The areosa race emerges from the Shadowlands. They are known mostly as rumors, but their existence is verified to the outside world.

209SA: Whether the faeli escaped the torments of the World Wound or were released, none know, but they were so twisted by the centuries of abuse that they have become more children of Malgrimm than Ghaeial

233SA: Under Ghaeial's wishes, the sylvan efflorah, existing as trees since even before the humans came to Esfah, picked up their roots and first emerged from forest and grove

829SA: Zephras "Thunderfist" dies defending in Cyrea defending Balgavarr from a dragon

967SA: Geril sa'Guhren "Dragonsbane" born

1021SA: Geril sa'Guhren rules in Balgavarr

1082SA: Coryn Sa'Geril is born

1119SA: Daybringer Comet makes its pass by Esfah

1122SA: Kholkoro Wicebrow writes her commentary *Kholkoro's commentary on Book of the Land*

1127SA: The famed "Adventurer King" Hy'Mander sa'Meril is blinded

1139SA: Melkior is revived

1142SA: Daybringer Comet makes its circuit

The Shadowlands
Icehome
Deep Woods
Iulgah
Mansjan Mountains
Baygarron
Thuria
Plains of Seuham
Plaguelands
Urutuk Mountains
Gyrea
Frostspear
Briney Main

# BOOKS
## IN THE DRAGON DICE UNIVERSE
## OF ESFAH

Rise and Fall of the Obsidian Grotto
Cast of Fate
Tome of Tarvenehl*
Heart of Stone and Flame*
Ashes of Ailushurai
Rise of the Champions
Drakuwar
Chill Wind
Eye of the Storm
Secrets of the Shadowlands
Army of the Dead**

*These two short books were the first produced by TSR and are included inside the re-released (2020) version of Cast of Fate, which was originally produced in 1996.

**This book was scheduled for release by TSR in the late 1990s but never published. A version of this book was released in 2003 but this version is not considered Esfah canon.

## About the authors:

Joseph W. Joiner (1965-2014) was born in Wichita, Kansas, to parents of Irish and Swedish descent. At age 5, his family relocated to Colorado Springs, Colorado, where he grew up in the shadow of America's mountain, Pikes Peak. He married his high-school sweetheart in 1986 and had two children, Jennifer Leigh and Jacob Ryan, before divorcing in 1994. He met his current wife, Paula, that same year and they married in 1995.

They had three children, Joseph Paul, Emily Shae, and Eleta Alexandra. He and his family lived in Colorado Springs, not far from the house where he grew up.

Joe was an avid board-game collector, and loved reading, seeing good movies, and riding his motorcycle through the mountains.

Chill Wind was his first published book, but he had plans for many more, including the sequel and prequel to Chill Wind and his science fiction epic that he has been working on for almost 20 years.

The sequel was later written by Christopher D. Schmitz and Sherif Guirgas. A prequel novellete titled *Thunderfist and the Dragon* was completed by Schmitz using snippets Joiner wrote for a previous SFR rules book; this story was released as bonus material in the re-release of *Cast of Fate* (2020).

Christopher D. Schmitz is author of both Sci-Fi/Fantasy Fiction and Nonfiction books and has been published in both traditional and independent outlets. If you've looked into indie writers of the upper midwest you may have heard his name whispered in dark alleys with an equal mix of respect and disdain. He has been featured on television broadcasts, podcasts, and runs a blog for indie authors… but you've still probably never heard of him.

As an avid consumer of comic books, movies, cartoons, and books (especially sci-fi and fantasy) this child of the 80s basically lived out Stranger Things, but shadowy government agencies won't let him say more than that. He lives in rural Minnesota with his family where he drinks unsafe amounts of coffee; the caffeine shakes keeps the cold from killing them. In his off-time he plays haunted bagpipes in places of low repute, but that's a story for another time.

He has a special offer for readers on the following page.

You can connect with him via the following links:
**http://www.authorchristopherdschmitz.com**

Follow me on Twitter:
https://twitter.com/cylonbagpiper
Follow me on Goodreads:
www.goodreads.com/author/show/129258.Christopher_Schmitz
Like/Follow me on Facebook:
https://www.facebook.com/authorchristopherdschmitz
Subscribe to my blog:
https://authorchristopherdschmitz.wordpress.com
Favorite me at Smashwords:
www.smashwords.com/profile/view/authorchristopherdschmitz
My amazon Author Profile:
amazon.com/author/christopherdschmitz
Follow me at Bookbub:
www.bookbub.com/authors/christopher-d-schmitz

# SPECIAL OFFER:

As a special bonus for you, I'd like to invite you download FIVE ebooks for free as a part of my Starter Library.

To get your free Starter Library, simply visit this link:
https://www.subscribepage.com/p1o9c9
Enter your email address and then collect your books as they are sent to you. It's that simple!

FREE STARTER BOOK LIBRARY

If you like Sci-Fi and Fantasy, you'll love these books, subscribe now to have them delivered right away.

Dragon Dice™ is SFR Inc.'s core product. We are constantly working to create a quality game that everyone can enjoy. Dragon Dice™ was originally created by Lester Smith and produced by TSR© in 1995. After several years, TSR, now owned by Wizards of the Coast, had put Dragon Dice™ on hold to work on other projects. In October of 2000, SFR Inc. purchased the rights to Dragon Dice™ and now will continue to support and create NEW! products for the game.

Dragon Dice™ is strategy game where players create mythical armies using dice to represent each troop. The game combines strategy and skill as well as a little luck. Each person tries to win the game by outmaneuvering the opponent and capture 2 terrains. Of course eliminating your opponent completely is another acceptable way of winning.

Get online today and "Roll your way to victory!"

http://www.sfr-inc.com